RED
LEAVES

ALSO BY THOMAS H. COOK

FICTION

Blood Innocents
The Orchids
Tabernacle
Elena
Sacrificial Ground
Flesh and Blood
Streets of Fire
Night Secrets
The City When It Rains
Evidence of Blood
Mortal Memory
Breakheart Hill
The Chatham School Affair
Instruments of Night
Places in the Dark
Interrogation
Taken (based on the teleplay by Leslie Boehm)
Moon over Manhattan (with Larry King)
Peril
Into the Web

NONFICTION

Early Graves
Blood Echoes
Best American Crime Writing: 2002 Edition (ed. with Otto Penzler)
Best American Crime Writing: 2003 Edition (ed. with Otto Penzler)
Best American Crime Writing: 2004 Edition (ed. with Otto Penzler)

RED
LEAVES

THOMAS H. COOK

AN OTTO PENZLER BOOK
A HARVEST BOOK • HARCOURT, INC.
Orlando Austin New York San Diego Toronto London

www.HarcourtBooks.com

The Library of Congress has cataloged the hardcover edition as follows:
Cook, Thomas H.
Red leaves/Thomas H. Cook.—1st ed.
p.   cm.
1.Fathers and sons—Fiction. 2. Missing children—Fiction
3. Teenage boys—Fiction. 4. Babysitters—Fiction.   I. Title.
PS3553.O55465R43 2005
813'.54—dc22   2004019782
ISBN-13: 978-0-15-101250-3   ISBN-10: 0-15-101250-4
ISBN-13: 978-0-15-603234-6 (pbk.)   ISBN-10: 0-15-603234-1 (pbk.)

Text set in AGaramond
Designed by Cathy Riggs

Printed in the United States of America

First Harvest edition 2006
A C E G I K J H F D B

For Susan Terner,
courage under fire

Oh, return to zero, the master said.
Use what's lying around the house.
Make it simple and sad.

—STEPHEN DUNN, *"Visiting the Master"*

PART I

When you remember those times, they return to you in a series of photographs. You see Meredith on the day you married her. You are standing outside the courthouse on a bright spring day. She is wearing a white dress and she stands beside you with her hand in your arm. A white corsage is pinned to her dress. You gaze at each other rather than the camera. Your eyes sparkle and the air around you is dancing.

Then there are the brief vacations before Keith was born. You are in a raft on the Colorado River, sprayed with white water. There you are, nearly blinded by the autumn foliage of New Hampshire. On the observation deck of the Empire State Building, you mug for the camera, feet spread, fists pressed to waists, like masters of the universe. You are twenty-four and she is twenty-one, and there is something gloriously confident in the way you stand together, sure and almost cocky. More than anything, without fear. Love, you have decided by then, is a form of armor.

Keith appears first in the crook of Meredith's right arm. She is lying in a hospital bed, her face bathed in sweat, her hair in disarray. Keith's small body floats in a swirl of bedding. His face is in profile, and a tiny pink hand instinctively reaches for something his closed eyes cannot see, his mother's loosely covered breast. Meredith is laughing at this gesture, but you recall that she was clearly struck by it, too, thought it a sign of high intelligence or early adventurousness, ambition, the drive to make a mark. You reminded her, joking, that her son was only a few minutes old. Yes, yes, of course, she said.

Here he is at two, unsteady on his feet, toddling toward the stuffed bear your brother, Warren, gave him that Christmas. Warren sits on the sofa, beside Meredith. He is leaning forward, his large pudgy hands blurred because he was clapping when you took the picture, clapping hard and fast, urging Keith forward like a good wind at his back. So lucky, Bro, he will say to you at the door before he leaves, so lucky to have all this.

You often pose before all you have. You stand with Meredith and Keith, who is six now and holds a plastic Wiffle ball bat. You are in front of the little house on Cranberry Way. You bought it on the slimmest of financial credentials, and Meredith predicted the loan would not be approved, and so, when it was, you uncorked a bottle of inexpensive champagne and toasted your new status as home-owners. There's the picture, you and Meredith with glasses raised,

Keith standing between you, his six-year-old hand lifted in imitation, holding a glass of apple juice.

You build a business, buy a second, larger, house on a more secluded lot. In that larger house the holidays come and go. You carve turkey and hang ornaments on real trees, then later, fearing fire, on artificial ones. In photographs you wallow in holiday gift wrapping, and as the years pass, the pictures show your face aglow in the light of many birthday candles.

You buy Meredith a ring on your fifteenth anniversary and with Keith and Warren watching, you marry her again, this time writing your own vows. That night, in the bed's comforting darkness, she tells you that she has never stopped loving you, and it is all you can do not to weep.

You buy your son a simple, inexpensive bike for his tenth birthday, then an elaborate twelve-speed when he turns fourteen. He's not particularly mechanical, so you spend some time showing him the gears. After a while, you ask him if he'd prefer a less-complicated bike. He says he would, but that it has nothing to do with the gears. He prefers everything less complicated, he tells you, and the look in his eyes when he says this suggests that there may be hidden depths in him, unexpected complexities. You say nothing of this, however, but later you wonder if your son, the one who'd once rested so securely in the crook of Meredith's arm, has now begun to emerge from the comfortable cocoon you have so carefully woven around him. If so, you are pleased, and you are sure Meredith will be pleased.

Another year passes. Keith is almost as tall as you are, and Meredith has never looked more radiant. A warm satisfaction settles over you, and you realize that it isn't the house or the business that fills you with a sense of accomplishment. It is your family, the depth and balance it has given to your life, a quiet rootedness and sense of well-being your father never attained and which, for some reason at the end of that summer, you recognize as the crowning victory of your life.

And so you decide to take a photograph. You set up the tripod and call Keith and Meredith outside. You take your place between them, one arm over your son, the other over your wife. You have timed the camera. You see the warning light and draw them close in beside you. Ready now, you tell them—smile.

ONE

F*amily photos always lie.*

That's what occurred to me when I left my house that final afternoon, and so I took only two.

The first was of my earliest family, when I was a son, rather than a father. In the picture, I am standing with my mother and father, along with my older brother, Warren, and my younger sister, Jenny. I am smiling, happy because I've just been accepted to a prestigious private day school. But the other smiles now strike me as false, because even then there must have been fissures in the unruffled happiness they convey, beasts lurking just beyond the firelight.

By the end of that summer, for example, my father must have known that years of bad investments and extravagant spending had surely caught up with him, that bankruptcy and its accompanying humiliations were only a few short months away. I doubt, however, that he could have envisioned the full bleakness of his final years, the retirement home where he would sit hour upon hour, peering through the lace curtains, thinking of the grand house in which we'd all once lived, another asset lost.

Despite all this, or maybe because of it, my father meets the camera with a broad and oddly blustering grin, as if the old man felt his smile could protect him from the horde of angry creditors that was already gathering for a final assault. My mother's smile is more tentative—weak, hesitant, like a translucent mask beneath which her true face, though blurred, is yet still visible. It is an effortful smile, the corners of her mouth lifted like heavy weights, and had I been less self-absorbed, I might have noticed its tentativeness earlier, perhaps in time to have asked the question that later repeated so insistently in my mind, *What is going on in you?*

But I never asked, and so the day her car went flying off Van Cortland Bridge, it never occurred to me that anything might have been on her mind other than what she planned to cook for dinner or the laundry she'd left neatly folded on all our beds that afternoon.

My brother, Warren, stands sloppily to my left. He is only fifteen, but his hair is already thinning and his belly is wide and round and droops over his belt. Even at that age, he looks curiously past his prime. He is smiling, of course, and there is no hint of any reason why he shouldn't be, though I later had to wonder what fears might even then have begun to surface, the sense that certain already-planted seeds would bear grim fruit.

Finally, there is Jenny, so beautiful that even at seven she turned heads when she came into a room. Adorable, Warren always called her. He'd stroke her hair or sometimes simply look at her admiringly. Adorable, he'd say. And she was. But she was also quick and knowing, a little girl who came home from her first day at school and asked me why it was necessary for the teacher to repeat things. I told her it was because some people couldn't get it the first time. She took this in for a moment, thinking quietly, as if trying to incorporate nature's inequality within the scheme of things, calculate its human toll. "How sad," she said finally, lifting those sea blue eyes toward me, "because it's not their fault."

In this particular photograph Jenny's smile is wide and unencumbered, though in all the photographs after this one the cloud is clearly visible, the knowledge that it has already taken root in that fantastic brain of hers, microscopic at first, then no larger than a pinpoint, but growing steadily, taking things from her as it grew, her balance, her ringing speech, everything but her beauty, before it took her life.

She was the one I most often thought about after leaving my house that last afternoon. I don't know why, save that I suspected she might be able to understand things better than I could, and so I wanted to go over it all with her, trace the burning fuse, its series of explosions, seek her celestial wisdom, ask her, *Do you think it had to end this way, Jenny, or might the damage have been avoided, the dead ones saved?*

The evening of that final death, he said, "I'll be back before the news." Meaning, I suppose, the network news, which meant that he would be home before six-thirty. There was no hint of the ominous in what he said, or of anything sinister, no sense at all that the center had collapsed.

When I recall that day, I think of my second family, the one in which I am husband to Meredith and father to Keith, and I wonder what I might have said or done to stop the red tide that overwhelmed us. That's when I see another picture, this one of a little girl from another family, a school photograph used in a hastily distributed flyer, the little girl smiling happily below the cold black words: MISSING.

Amy Giordano.

She was the only daughter of Vince and Karen Giordano. Vince owned a modest produce market just outside the town limits. It was called Vincent's Fresh Food, and Vince dressed himself as a walking advertisement for the place. He wore green flannel pants, a green vest, and a green cap, the latter two articles festooned with the name of the store. He was a short muscular man with the look of a high school wrestler who'd let himself go, and the last time I saw him—before the night Keith left for his house—he was carrying a brown paper bag with six rolls of film. "My brother's family came for a week," he explained as he handed me the bag, "and his wife, she's a camera nut."

I owned a small camera and photo shop in the town's only strip mall, and the pictures Vincent Giordano left that afternoon showed two families, one large, with at least four children ranging in age from approximately four to twelve, and which had to have belonged to the visiting brother and his "camera nut" wife. The other family was small, a circle of three—Vince, his wife, Karen, and Amy, their only daughter.

In the pictures, the two families present themselves in poses that anyone who develops family photos taken at the end of summer in a small coastal town would expect. They are lounging in lawn chairs or huddled around outdoor tables, eating burgers and hotdogs. Sometimes they sprawl on brightly colored beach towels or stand on the gangway of chartered fishing boats. They smile and seem happy and give every indication that they have nothing to hide.

I have since calculated that Vincent dropped off his six rolls of film during the last week of August, less than a month before that fateful Friday evening when he and Karen went out to dinner. Just the two of them, as he later told police. Just the two of them . . . without Amy.

Amy always reminded me of Jenny. And it was more than her looks, the long wavy hair I saw in her family photos, the deep-blue eyes and luminous white skin. Certainly Amy was beautiful, as Jenny had been beautiful. But in the photographs there is a similar sense of intuitiveness. You looked into Amy's eyes and you thought that she saw—as Jenny did—everything. To reporters, Detective Peak described her as "very bright and lively," but she was more than that. She had Jenny's way of peering at things for a long time, as if studying their structures. She did this the last time I saw her. On that September afternoon, Karen had brought in yet another few rolls of film, and while I wrote up the order, Amy moved about the store, carefully examining what she found there, the small, mostly digital, cameras I stocked, along with various lenses, light meters, and carrying cases. At one point she picked up one of the cameras and turned it over in her small white hands. It was an arresting scene, this beautiful child lost in thoughtful examination, silent, curiously intense, probing. Watching her, I had a sense that she was studying the camera's various mechanisms, its buttons and switches and dials. Most kids start by merely snapping pictures and grinning playfully, but the look on Amy's face was the look of a scientist or technician, an observer of materials and mechanical functions. She didn't want to take a picture; she wanted to discover how it was done.

"She was so special," Karen Giordano told reporters, words often used by parents to describe their children. As a description it is usually exaggerated, since the vast majority of children are not special at all, save in the eyes of those who love them. But that doesn't matter. What matters is that she was Karen Giordano's daughter. And so on those days when I make my way down the village street, noting faces that from high above might appear indistinguishable as grains of sand, I accept the notion that to someone down here, someone close up, each face is unique. It is a mother's face or a father's; a sister's or a brother's; a daughter's or a son's. It is a face upon which a thousand memories have been etched and so it is differentiated from every other face. This is the core of all attachment, the quality that makes us human, and if we did not have it we would swim forever in an indifferent sea, glassy-eyed and unknowing, seeking only the most basic sustenance. We would know the pain of teeth in our flesh and the stinging scrape of rocks and coral. But we would know nothing of devotion and thus nothing of Karen Giordano's anguish, the full measure of feeling that was hers, the irreparable harm and irrevocable loss, the agony and violence that lay secreted, as we all would come to learn, within a simple promise to be home before the news.

TWO

There was little rain that summer, and so when I heard the rumble of thunder, I looked up but saw nothing more threatening than a few high clouds, torn and ragged, pale brushstrokes across the blue.

"Heat lightning," I said.

Meredith nodded from her place in the hammock, but kept her attention on the magazine she was reading. "By the way," she said, "I have a departmental meeting tonight."

"On a Friday?" I asked.

She shrugged. "My thought, exactly, but Dr. Mays says we have to take a look at the year ahead. Make sure we understand our goals, that sort of thing."

For the last eight years, Meredith had taught in the English department of the local junior college. For most of that time, she'd served as a lowly adjunct. Then suddenly, death had opened a full-time position, and since then, she'd assumed more and more administrative duties, gone off on professional days and attended seminars in Boston and New York. She had grown more confident and self-assured with each added responsibility, and when I think of her now, it seems to me that she had never appeared happier than she did that evening, relaxed and unburdened, a woman who'd found the balance of family and career that best suited her.

"I should be home by ten," she said.

I was standing at the brick grill I'd built four summers before, an unnecessarily massive structure I enjoyed showing off for the loving craft I'd employed while building it. There were brick curves and brick steps and little brick shelves, and I loved the sheer solidity of it, the way it would hold up against even the strongest storm. I'd also loved every aspect of the work, the thick, wet feel of the mortar and the heaviness of the brick. There was nothing flimsy about it, nothing frail or tentative or collapsible. It was, Meredith later told me, a metaphor not for how things were, but for how I wanted them, everything lined up evenly, made of materials that were sturdy and unbending, built to last.

Our house, when I think of it now, had that same determined sturdiness. It was built of ancient wood, rough-hewn and very nearly petrified. The living-room ceiling rose at a forty-five-degree angle, supported by thick beams, and at the end of it there was a fireplace of gray stone. The grounds were also incontestably the product of a mind that sought security. The yard was thick with trees and wild brush that made it impossible to see the house from the road. An unpaved drive wound in a long lazy circle to the front of the house, then lifted up a short hill and circled back to the main road. It was possible to make the turn into the driveway and immediately disappear into densely covering forest. Save for that one break in the trees, no one would even have suspected that a family lived nearby. We lived on a desert island, as Meredith once said, in the middle of the woods.

I'd put on a couple of extra burgers because Warren had called earlier, sounding tired from his long day of house painting. I knew he hated spending Friday night alone, so I'd invited him over for a cookout. In recent weeks, he'd begun to drink more, and his fleeting efforts to "find the right woman" had declined both in number and intensity. The year before he'd fallen off a ladder while repairing a patch of rotted shingles on the small two-story house he rented. The fall had broken his hip and he'd been laid up for nearly a month. There'd been no one to look after him, no wife or children, and so he'd moved into Keith's room for his convalescence, a period during which he'd played computer games and watched videos, usually adventure movies because, as he put it with a soft, self-mocking smile, "I have a lot to keep my mind off of."

He arrived at just before five, moving sluggishly up the winding walkway that led to the grill. Around him, in the lowering sun, the leaves were so brilliantly colored that he seemed to walk through a shimmering oil painting. The foliage had always been spectacular, but I most admired the Japanese maple I'd planted at the end of the walkway, its graceful branches, laden with red leaves, spread out like enveloping arms that seemed to draw you into its protective care.

"So, how's the chef?" Warren asked as he plopped down in a lawn chair a few feet from Meredith.

Meredith put down her magazine. "He's only the summer chef," she said lightly. "He doesn't lift a finger when he's not at that grill." She pulled herself out of the hammock. "Got to get dressed," she said, then bounded into the house.

"Dressed for what?" Warren asked.

"Department meeting," I said.

The phone rang inside the house, and through the front window I saw Keith rush to pick it up, his movement considerably more sprightly than normal, so that I briefly sensed that the person at the other end might be the long-awaited girlfriend he'd no doubt been pining for. He talked briefly, then put the phone down and came to the door.

"Okay if I babysit tonight?" he asked. "Mrs. Giordano can't get her usual one."

I knew that Karen Giordano usually employed Beth Carpenter to babysit when she and Vince went out, but she sometimes called Keith when Beth wasn't available. He had filled in four or five times before that night, always home before eleven, usually with some story about Amy, how bright and well-behaved she was, deserving of the name he'd given her— Princess Perfect.

"You caught up with your homework?" I asked.

"Except algebra," Keith said. "Besides, it's Friday, Dad. I have the whole weekend." He frowned as if I'd missed a cue. "So, can I?"

I shrugged. "Okay."

Keith returned inside, where I glimpsed him through the

window once again, speaking into the phone, a tall lanky boy of fifteen with a mop of curly black hair and skin so pale and soft to the touch it seemed very nearly feminine.

"You got a good kid there, Eric," Warren said. He glanced over at the grill. "Smells good."

We gathered around the picnic table a few minutes later. Meredith was dressed in her professorial attire, complete with a silk scarf and black pumps with a modestly high heel. Keith wore his usual jeans and sweatshirt along with the pair of worn tennis shoes he usually wore unlaced.

I remember that the conversation was rather limited that evening. I mentioned a roll of film I'd developed that morning, twenty-four pictures of the same goldfish. Meredith said that she'd come to like Dylan Thomas more than in the past, particularly his poem about a little girl who'd died by fire in London. "He was asked to write a poem about this one little girl," she said, "but refused to do that and wrote something universal instead."

Warren mostly complained that his hip still bothered him and that he might well require surgery in a year or two. He had always been one who needed sympathy, and sought it, the kind of man you'd think had been orphaned in his youth and thus was forever in search of a sweet maternal hand. My father had always found him soft and without ambition, called him "day labor" behind his back, and warned my mother not to baby him, one of the few of his commands she had had the will to disobey.

As for Keith, he seemed even more quiet than usual, his head low over his plate, as if vaguely ashamed to look us in the eye. He had always been a shy boy, awkward and withdrawn, prone to injury, and with an early dislike of physical contact. He'd shunned sports, but not out of regard for some other activity, playing a musical instrument, for example, or because of some interest or hobby, but only because he seemed wary of being touched. But more than anything, he gave off a sense of something enclosed, drawn in upon itself, disinclined to reach out.

Meredith had more than once asked if I thought Keith should see someone. I was not averse to such a suggestion, but at the same time I had no idea whom Keith might see. And of course, the real question, it seemed to me, was not whether he was involved in sports or had friends, but whether he was or wasn't happy. But I had no way of knowing this, and so I let him drift, the first years of his adolescence passing quietly, almost silently, until they reached the end of that summer, and he sat, hunched over his plate, while Meredith raced to her meeting and Warren slumped in the hammock and I cleared the table and cleaned the grill.

"So, you gonna take me?" Keith asked as he came out of the house, now dressed for that cool autumn evening in khaki pants, wool shirt, and blue parka.

"You look very handsome," I said.

He groaned, "Yeah, right."

"No, I mean it, you're growing into—"

He lifted his hand to stop me. "So, you gonna take me?"

Before I could answer, Warren struggled out of the hammock. "Let your father finish up, I'll take you."

And so they left, my brother and my son, the two of them

moving down the brick walkway through a dusky light, one wide and flabby, the other razor thin and erect, cutting through the air like a blade.

When they were gone I finished the cleaning, carefully scrubbed the grill's charred ironwork, then walked inside the house. Meredith had left a book on the table, *The Collected Poems of Dylan Thomas*. I picked it up, brought it over to my chair, and switched on the gooseneck lamp. Then I opened the book, looked up the poem she'd talked about at dinner, found it hard to follow, but interesting enough, especially the mournful sentiment at the end, that, according to the poet, "After the first death, there is no other."

I was snoozing in my chair when the phone rang a few hours later.

It was Keith. "You don't have to pick me up," he said. "I'm gonna stay out for a while. Maybe hang out with some people."

I'd never known Keith simply to seek out other people, but given his troubling solitariness, the news that he might have such an urge struck me as an encouraging sign of normality.

"So, when will you be in?" I asked.

"I don't know," Keith answered. "Before . . . midnight, okay?"

"Okay," I said. "But no later. Your mother would be worried."

"Okay, Dad," Keith said.

He hung up and I went back to my chair, though not to *The Collected Poems of Dylan Thomas*. I had never had partic-

ularly refined taste in literature, although the occasional serious novel might gain a little ground among the nonfiction
that was my usual fare. On this particular night, it was a book
about an African tribe that had been displaced, moved from a
region in which the tribesmen had been farmers to one in
which they were reduced to gathering food among the sparse
foliage that dotted otherwise rocky, inhospitable soil. As their
condition had grown more desperate, their ancient religious
and social institutions had collapsed. All that had once seemed
so firm crumbled, all their habits and relations—everything.
There was no solid human nature, the book said, there were
only met and unmet needs, our deepest roots sunk in shifting
sand.

I had just finished the book when Meredith returned home.

She seemed surprised that I hadn't gone to bed.

"Keith called," I told her. "He's going to be late."

Meredith dropped her purse on the sofa and began pulling
off her shoes. "The Giordanos are making a late night of it, I
guess."

"No, he's already left there," I told her. "He said he might
hang out with some people."

She cocked her head quizzically. "Well, that's an interesting development. Or it will be, if it's true."

Her final words struck me as unexpectedly suspicious.

"True?" I asked. "Why wouldn't it be true?"

She came over and touched my face, her gaze oddly in-
dulgent, as if explaining life to a little boy. "Because people lie,
Eric."

"But why else would he be out?" I asked.

She shrugged. "Maybe he's buying drugs," she said jokingly. "Or maybe he's a Peeping Tom."

I laughed, and so did she, since the image of our son lurking in the shadows, peering into windows, seemed comical, one of the many things we could not imagine him doing.

"I told him to be back home by midnight," I said.

She reached for me. "Let's go to bed," she said.

Meredith often tossed restlessly for hours before finally dropping off, but that night was different. She fell asleep right away, like someone exhausted by a long day's labor. For a time, I watched her, pleased with how smart and lovely she was, how contented with the life we shared. By then, many of our friends had divorced, and those who hadn't seemed hardly better off, either snippy with one another or dismissive, the pleasure they'd once taken together now no more than a distant memory.

We'd met during her last year of college, dated for six months, then married. We'd lived in Boston for a time, where she'd taught at a local public school while I'd worked at a pharmaceutical company. We'd both hated our jobs, and so, a few months after Keith came along, we'd taken the plunge, moved to Wesley, managed to secure a loan, and bought the frame and photo shop. Meredith had stayed home with Keith for the first seven years, then taken a part-time teaching job at the junior college. As Keith grew older, she'd added to her teaching load, shedding her former household duties like a dry skin, becoming younger and more vibrant, it seemed to me, so that as she slept that night, it did not surprise me that her lips suddenly lifted in a quiet smile.

I was peering at that smile when I heard a car crunch to a halt at the far end of the drive. I sat up in bed, and glanced out the window. By then the car was backing onto the road, two beams of light sweeping across the undergrowth with a smooth, ghostly grace. Seconds later I saw Keith make his way down the unpaved drive that circled around to our front door, his pace slow and halting, head down as if against a hostile wind.

After a moment, he disappeared from view. Then I heard the metallic click of the front door, the sound of his feet as he made his way up the stairs, past our bedroom, and down the corridor to his own room.

He was just opening the door to that room when I stepped into the hallway.

"Hi," I said.

He didn't turn toward me, but stood, facing the door, his body curiously stiff.

"Did you have a good time with your friends?" I asked lightly.

He nodded, the long strands of his hair shifting in a tangled curtain as he moved.

"Good," I said.

As he eased around to face me, I saw that his shirttail was rumpled, as if it had been hurriedly tucked in. "Okay if I go to bed now?" he asked a little curtly, but with no more than the usual teenage impatience.

"Yes," I said. "I just wanted to make sure you were okay."

He quickly turned and disappeared into his room, leaving me alone in the dimly lit corridor.

I returned to my bed, now fully awake, feeling an inexplicable unease, a sense that something in the nature of things had quietly turned against me, undermining my long certitude, as if, beneath the house's firm foundation, I could feel a subtle trembling in the earth.

THREE

The next morning Meredith was already up and making breakfast by the time I came into the kitchen.

"Well, hello, sleepyhead," she said lightly.

The air was thick with the salty smell of bacon and brewing coffee, odors that mark a family man as surely as cheap perfume betrays a bounder.

"You're awfully energetic this morning," I said.

Meredith forked a strip of bacon onto a paper towel to let it drain. "I woke up starving. Don't you ever wake up starving?"

For some reason, I heard a faint sense of accusation in her question, the sense that my own early-morning lack of appetite was emblematic of deeper deficiencies. Did I lack ambition, too, she seemed to ask. And passion? Did I lack sufficient hungers?

She drew the bacon from the paper towel and took a

quick bite. "Yum." She snapped at the dangling end of the bacon, tearing the meat away in small bites. Wolfishly. I half expected to hear her growl.

Or did she do any of this, I wonder now. Was it merely something I thought I saw? And even if it were really there, where does a man go with such odd presentiments, a sense, vague and ineffable, that you do not really know the one you know, that all your previous soundings have gone no deeper than the shallows.

I sat down at the table, picked up the paper, and glanced at the headline, something about the proposed town budget. "Keith got in late." I idly turned the page, now looking for the ad I'd placed three days before. "Around midnight, I guess."

Meredith grabbed the pot from the coffeemaker and poured each of us a steaming cup.

"I heard him come in," I added. "But you were out like a light."

She sat down, took a sip from her cup, then tossed her hair with an earthy flare, like a woman in a roadhouse. "Beautiful morning," she said. Then she laughed.

"What's so funny?"

"Oh, just some silly joke Dr. Mays told us at the meeting."

"Which was?"

She waved her hand. "You wouldn't think it was funny."

"Why do you say that?"

"It's silly, Eric. You wouldn't like it."

"Try me."

She shrugged. "Okay," she said, "It wasn't really a joke. It was a quotation. From Lenny Bruce." She chuckled again.

"He said that the difference between a man and a woman is that when a woman is thrown through a plateglass window, she doesn't get up thinking about sex."

"Dr. Mays said that?" I asked, surprised. "Dr. Mays of the thick glasses and tweed jacket and white meerschaum pipe?"

Meredith took another sip of coffee. "The very one."

I folded the paper and laid it on the table. "I'm surprised he's even heard of Lenny Bruce."

Meredith snapped another strip of bacon from the plate and took a small bite. "People aren't always what they seem," she said.

"Not me." I spread out my arms. "I'm exactly what I seem."

She started to respond, then caught herself and said, "Yes, you are, Eric. You are exactly what you seem."

Again, I felt the hint of an accusation of being flat, one-dimensional, by-the-book, dully transparent. I thought of my father, the mystery man, his unexplained absences from and abrupt returns to the family circle, his empty chair at the dining table, the vacant look in my mother's eyes when they inadvertently fell upon it. I drew my arms back in. "And that's a good thing, right?" I asked.

"What's a good thing?" Meredith asked.

"Being what I seem," I answered. "Because otherwise you might be afraid of me."

"Afraid?"

"That I might suddenly become someone else. A murderer or something. One of those guys who comes home from work one day and hacks his whole family to death."

Meredith appeared faintly alarmed. "Don't say things like

that, Eric." Her eyes darted away, then returned to me, sparkling darkly, as if the tables had been turned, and she had spotted the animal in me.

"I'm just making a point," I told her. "If people really weren't what they seemed, then we could never trust each other, and if that happened, the whole thing would fall apart, wouldn't it?"

She turned my question over in her mind and seemed to come to some conclusion about it, though she gave no hint of what the conclusion was. Instead, she rose, walked to the sink, and looked out across the grounds, her eyes darting from the picnic table to the grill before settling on the wooden bird feeder, which hung from a nearby pine. "Winter's coming," she said. "I hate winter."

This was not a sentiment she'd ever expressed before. "Hate winter? I thought you loved winter. The fire, the coziness."

She looked at me. "You're right. I guess it's autumn I don't like."

"Why?"

She returned her gaze to the window. Her right hand lifted, as if on its own, a pale bird rising until it came to rest at her throat. "I don't know," she said. "Maybe just all those falling leaves."

A few of those leaves had already fallen, I noticed, as I headed down the walkway to my car. They were large and yellow, with small brown spots that looked vaguely disturbing, like tiny cancers in the flesh of the leaf.

Which is probably why I thought of Jenny as I continued

down the walkway that morning. I couldn't imagine the icy tremor that had surely coursed through my mother and father when the doctor had first diagnosed the tumor. Or maybe it had felt like a blade, slicing them open, spilling any hope of future happiness onto the tiled floor. Jenny, the bright one, the one with the most promise, was going to die, and so there would be no family photographs of her growing up, acting in the school play, graduating, going to college, marrying, having children of her own. That was what must have struck them at that instant, I decided, that the life they'd expected, both Jenny's and their own, had just exploded, leaving nothing but acrid smoke behind.

I'd reached the car and was about to get in when I saw Meredith open the front door, her arm outstretched, waving me back toward the house.

"What is it?" I called.

She said nothing, but continued to wave, so I closed the door and returned to the house.

"It's Vince Giordano," she said, nodding toward the kitchen phone.

I looked at her quizzically, then went to the phone. "Hey, Vince," I said.

"Eric," Vince said starkly. "Listen, I didn't want to upset Meredith, but I have to know if you . . . if you've seen Keith this morning."

"No, I haven't. He usually sleeps late on Saturday morning."

"But he's home? He came home last night?"

"Yes, he did."

"Do you know when that was?"

Suddenly, I felt my answer assume unexpected weight. "Around midnight, I think."

There was a brief silence, then Vince said, "Amy's missing."

I waited for Vince to finish the sentence, tell me what Amy was missing, a ring, a watch, something Keith could help her find.

"She wasn't in her room this morning," Vince added. "We waited for her to get up and come down, but she never did. So we went up to look . . . and she was . . . gone."

I would later remember Vince's words not so much as words, but as a distant tolling, accompanied by a palpable change in the weight of the air around me.

"We've looked everywhere," Vince added. "All over the house. The neighborhood. We can't find her anywhere, and so I thought maybe . . . Keith . . ."

"I'll get him up," I said quickly. "I'll call you right back."

"Thanks," Vince said softly. "Thank you."

I hung up and glanced toward Meredith. She read the expression on my face and looked suddenly troubled.

"It's Amy," I told her. "They can't find her. She wasn't in her room this morning. They've looked everywhere, but so far, nothing."

"Oh, no," Meredith whispered.

"We have to talk to Keith."

We walked upstairs together. I tapped at Keith's door. No answer. I tapped again. "Keith?"

There was still no answer and so I tried the door. As always, it was locked. I tapped again, this time much more loudly. "Keith, get up. This is important."

I heard a low moan, then the pad of Keith's feet as he walked to the door. "What is it?" he groaned without opening it.

"It's about Amy Giordano," I said. "Her father just called. They can't find her."

The door opened slightly and a watery eye seemed to swim toward me like a small blue fish through the murky water of an aquarium.

"Can't find her?" Keith asked.

"That's what I said."

Meredith pressed near the door. "Get dressed and come downstairs, Keith," she said. Her voice was quite stern, like a teacher's. "Hurry up."

We walked back downstairs and sat at the kitchen table and waited for Keith to come join us.

"Maybe she just went for a walk," I said.

Meredith looked at me worriedly. "If something happened to Amy, Keith would be the one they'd suspect."

"Meredith, there's no point in—"

"Maybe we should call Leo."

"Leo? No. Keith doesn't need a lawyer."

"Yes, but—"

"Meredith, all we're going to do is ask Keith a few questions. When he last saw Amy. If she seemed okay. Then I'm going to call Vince and tell him what Keith said." I looked at her pointedly. "Okay?"

She nodded tensely. "Yes, fine."

Keith slouched down the stairs, still drowsy, scratching his head. "Now . . . what did you say about Amy?" he asked, as he slumped down in a chair at the kitchen table.

"She's missing," I told him.

Keith rubbed his eyes with his fists. "That's crazy," he said, with a light, dismissive grunt.

Meredith leaned forward, her voice measured. "This is serious, Keith. Where was Amy when you left the Giordanos' house last night?"

"In her bedroom," Keith answered, still drowsy, but now coming a bit more to life. "I read her a story. Then I went to the living room and watched TV."

"When did you read her the story?"

"About eight-thirty, I guess."

"Don't guess," Meredith snapped. "Don't guess about anything, Keith."

For the first time the gravity of the situation registered on Keith's face. "She's really missing?" he asked, as if everything up to now had been some kind of joke.

"What do you think we've been saying, Keith?" Meredith asked.

"Listen," I said to him. "I want you to think carefully, because I have to call Mr. Giordano and tell him exactly what you tell me. So, like your mother says, Keith, don't guess about anything."

He nodded, and I could see that it had sunk in fully now. "Okay, sure," he said.

"All right," I began. "You didn't see Amy again, right? Not after you read her that story?"

"No."

"Are you sure?"

"Yes," Keith answered emphatically. His gaze darted over to Meredith. "I didn't see her again."

"Do you have any idea where she is?" I asked.

Keith looked suddenly offended. "Of course not." He glanced back and forth between Meredith and me. "It's the truth," he cried. "I didn't see her again."

"Did you see anything?" I asked.

"What do you mean?"

"Anything out of the ordinary."

"You mean like . . . was she acting funny . . . or—"

"Funny. Strange. Unhappy. Maybe wanting to run away? Did she give you any hint of that?"

"No."

"Okay, how about something else," I said. "Somebody around the house. Peeping Tom, that sort of thing."

Keith shook his head. "I didn't see anything, Dad." His eyes swept over to Meredith, and I saw the first suggestion of worry in them. "Am I in trouble?"

Meredith sat back slightly, the posture she always assumed when she had no immediate answer.

Keith held his gaze on Meredith. "Are the police going to talk to me?"

Meredith shrugged. "I guess it depends."

"On what?"

Meredith remained silent.

Keith looked at me. "On what, Dad?"

I gave him the only answer I had. "On what happened to Amy, I suppose."

FOUR

Later I would try to define it, the uneasiness of those first few minutes. I would go over the phone call from Vince, the way Meredith and I had trudged up the stairs together then returned to the kitchen and waited for Keith. I would try to remember if I'd heard something during that otherwise silent interval, the sound of tiny insect teeth or a steady drip of water, small, insistent, relentlessly undermining. Now I know the chasm that yawned beneath the lives we had so carefully constructed. I hear a gunshot, a resigned murmur, and in those sounds all I didn't know flashes clear and bright.

But what *did* I know? The answer is clear. I knew nothing. And what do you do when you know nothing? You take the next step because you have to and because, in your ignorance, you can't possibly know how blind it is, the step you're taking, or how dire its unseen consequences.

And so after Keith returned to his room, I simply called Vince Giordano and told him exactly what my son had said, half believing that that might be the end of it for Keith, Meredith, and me, that whatever terrible thing might have happened to Amy Giordano, her spilled blood, if it had been spilled, would not wash over the rest of us.

"I'm sorry, Vince," I said. "I wish I could be more help, but Keith simply has no idea where Amy is."

After a pause, Vince said, "I have to ask you something."

"Anything."

"Did Keith leave the house while he was here with Amy?"

I had no way of knowing if Keith had left Vince's house at any point during the time he'd been there, but I suddenly felt the need to answer anyway, and so I gave an answer I deeply hoped was true.

"I'm sure he didn't," I said.

"Would you mind asking him?" Vince's voice was almost pleading. "We just can't figure out what happened."

"Of course," I told him.

"Just ask him if he left Amy . . . even for a minute," Vince repeated.

"I'll call you right back," I said, then hung up and walked up the stairs, leaving Meredith alone and looking increasingly worried at the kitchen table.

Keith's door was closed but he opened it at my first tap,

though slightly, so that only half his face was visible, a single eye peering at me through a narrow slit.

"Mr. Giordano wants to know if you left the house at any point last night," I said.

The eye blinked languidly, like a curtain drawn down slowly then reluctantly raised.

"Well, did you?"

"No," Keith answered.

It was a firm no, and yet his answer had come only after a moment of hesitation, or was it calculation?

"Are you sure about that, Keith?" I asked.

This time his answer came without hesitation. "Yes."

"Absolutely sure? Because I have to go back now and tell Mr. Giordano."

"I didn't leave the house," Keith assured me.

"It's not a big deal if you did, Keith. It's not the same as if you—"

"As if I what, Dad?" Keith asked, almost snappishly.

"You know what I mean," I told him.

"As . . . if I killed her?" Keith asked. "Or whatever happened."

"I don't believe you did anything to Amy Giordano, if that's what you're accusing me of," I told him.

"Really?" Keith replied. His tone was petulant. "It sounds like you do. Mom, too. Like both of you think I did something."

"It only sounds that way to you, Keith," I said, my tone now changing with his, becoming suddenly defensive. "As a matter of fact, I told Mr. Giordano that you didn't leave the house before I came up here."

Keith didn't look as if he believed me, but he kept his doubts to himself.

"Anyway, I have to call Mr. Giordano back now," I said, then turned and quickly made my way down the stairs, Keith's door slamming sharply behind me, hard and unforgiving as a slap.

Karen Giordano answered the phone.

"Karen, it's Eric Moore."

"Oh, hello, Eric," Karen said with a slight sniffle that made me think she'd been crying.

"Has anything changed?" I asked.

"No," she answered. Her voice was weak. "We don't know where she is." She was ordinarily a cheerful woman, but all her cheer had drained away. "We've called everybody," Karen continued. "All the neighbors. Everybody." Her voice softened still more and took on an oddly pleading quality, so that it struck me that dread was a kind of humility, an admission of one's helplessness, the fact that, in the end, we control nothing. "No one's seen her."

I wanted to assure her that everything would turn out fine, that Amy would suddenly appear out of a closet or from behind a curtain, shout "April Fool" or something of the kind. But I had seen too many news stories to believe such a thing was likely. They really did vanish, these little girls, and if they were found at all, it was almost always too late. Still, there was one possibility. "Do you think that she could have . . . well . . . could be maybe trying to . . . make a point?"

"A point?" Karen asked.

"A statement," I added, then realized that the word was ridiculously formal. "Maybe, that she wants you to miss her so she—"

"Ran away?" Karen interrupted.

"Something like that," I said. "Kids can do crazy things."

She started to speak, but suddenly Vince was on the line. "What'd Keith say?" he asked urgently.

"He said he didn't leave the house."

Vince released a sigh. "Well, if that's what he says, then I have to call the police, Eric."

"Okay," I answered.

There was a pause, and I got the feeling that Vince was giving me, and perhaps my son, one last chance. So that's where we are now, I thought, he believes my son did something terrible to his daughter and there's nothing I can do to convince him otherwise, nothing I can say about Keith that he won't think tainted by my own protective fatherhood. Before I was a neighbor, a fellow tradesmen in a friendly town, someone he did business with and waved to and smiled at. But now I am an accessory to my son's imagined crime.

"I think you *should* tell the police, Vince."

It surprised me that my response appeared to take him aback, as if he'd expected me to argue against it.

"They'll want to talk to Keith," Vince warned.

"I'm sure he'll be happy to talk to them."

"Okay," Vince said, his tone strangely deflated, like a man forced to do something he'd hoped to avoid.

"Vince," I began, "if I can help in any—"

"Right," Vince interrupted. "I'll be in touch."

And with that, he hung up.

"That's all Vince said?" Meredith asked, as she walked me to the car a few minutes later. "That he would be in touch?"

We brushed passed the Japanese maple, a gentle pink light filtering through its leaves.

"And that he's calling the police," I said.

"He thinks Keith did something."

"Probably," I admitted.

Meredith remained silent until we reached the car. Then she said, "I'm afraid, Eric."

I touched her face. "We can't get ahead of ourselves. I mean, there's no proof that anything has—"

"Are you sure you don't want to call Leo?"

I shook my head. "Not yet."

I opened the door of the car and pulled myself in behind the wheel, but made no effort to leave. Instead, I rolled down the window and looked at my wife in a way that later struck me as shockingly nostalgic, as if she were already drifting away or changing in some way, these the dwindling days of our previously unencumbered life together. For a moment everything that had gone before, the best years of our lives, seemed precariously balanced, happiness a kind of arrogance, a bounty we had taken for granted until then, death the only clear and present danger, and even that still very far away. And yet, despite such dark presentiments, I said, "It's going to be okay, Meredith. It really is."

I could see she didn't believe me, but that was not unusual for Meredith. She had always been a worrier, concerned about money before things got really tight, keeping a close eye on even Keith's most petty delinquencies, forever poised to nip something in the bud. I had countered with optimism, looking on the bright side, a pose I still thought it necessary to maintain.

"We can't go off the deep end," I told her. "Even if something happened to Amy, it has nothing to do with us."

"That doesn't matter," Meredith said.

"Of course it does."

"No, it doesn't," Meredith said, "because once something like this happens, once they start asking questions . . ."

"But Keith didn't leave the house until the Giordanos came home," I said emphatically. "So it doesn't matter about the questions. He'll have the answers."

She drew in a long breath. "Okay, Eric," she said with a thin, frail smile. "Whatever you say."

She turned and headed back toward the house, a cool gust of wind sweeping the ground before her, fierce and devilish, kicking up those stricken yellow leaves I'd seen an hour earlier so that they spiraled up and up to where I saw Keith at his bedroom window, staring down at me, his gaze cold and resentful, as if I were no longer his father at all, no longer his protector or benefactor, but instead arrayed against him, part of the assembling mob that soon would be crying for his head.

"Morning," Neil said, as I came into the store.

It was nearly nine, so I knew he'd already prepped the developers and dusted the stock. He was thorough and reliable in that way, the perfect employee. Best of all, he gave no indication of having any larger ambition than to work in my shop, collect his small salary, and indulge his few modest pleasures. Twice a year he went to New York to take in four or five Broadway shows, usually the big musicals whose glitzy numbers clearly thrilled him. While there, he stayed at a small inexpensive hotel in Chelsea, ate street food, save for his final night when he splurged on Italian, and usually came back with a new snow globe to add to his collection of travel mementos. Briefly he'd had a partner named Gordon, a round, bearded man who often appeared in community theater presentations, though only as a bit player, listed in the program as "neighbor" or "prison guard." During the two years of their relationship, Neil's frame of mind had been closely tied to Gordon's severe mood swings, gloomy or cheerful depending, or so it often seemed, on the course of whatever show Gordon happened to be in at the time. Inevitably, they'd broken up, and since then Neil had lived with his ailing mother in a small house on one of the town's few remaining unpaved roads, an arrangement with which he seemed perfectly content, since, as he'd once told me, "anything else would require too much effort."

"Running late, boss," Neil added.

I nodded silently.

Neil cocked his head to the right. "Uh-oh, bad morning."

"A little," I admitted.

"Well, you'll perk up once the money starts rolling in. Speaking of which, I should probably go to the bank. We're low on change."

He left a few minutes later, and while I went about the usual preopening routine, restocking shelves, a quick sweep of the sidewalk outside the shop, I thought about Amy Giordano and how Vince seemed determined to lay the blame for whatever had happened to her at Keith's door.

But there was nowhere to go with such thoughts. I had no idea what had befallen Amy, whether she'd run away or suffered some monstrous fate. And so I retreated to the refuge I usually sought when I was feeling uneasy about money or Keith's grades or any of a hundred other petty troubles.

It was at the rear of the store, my little refuge, no more than a large table, really, along with a square of particle board hung with a modest assortment of stained-wood frames. Little skill was needed to frame the family photos that came my way. Usually people chose colors they thought appropriate to the scene: blue for families on the beach; greens and reds for families in forest encampments; gold or silver for families posed beside the tall sea grass that adorns the nearby bay; white for photos taken while whale watching.

Framing these smiling, bucolic scenes never failed to relax and reassure me. But a frame is just a frame, and the life it holds is frozen, static, beyond the reach of future events. Real life is another matter.

The phone rang.

It was Meredith. "Eric, come home," she told me.

"Why?" I asked.

"Because," she said, "they're here."

FIVE

There were two of them, both dressed in dark suits, a tall, hawk-faced man named Kraus, and another, shorter and rounder, whose name was Peak. They were sitting in the living room when I arrived, and both smiled pleasantly as they introduced themselves.

"I understand," Kraus began, "that Mr. Giordano called you this morning?"

"Yes."

We were all standing, Kraus's dark deep-set eyes leveled directly upon me; Peak a little to my left, seemed more interested, or so it seemed, in a family portrait I'd taken four years before, the three of us posed before Keith's sixth-grade science project, a plaster of paris sculpture of the body's internal organs, red heart, blue lungs, brown liver, and so on.

"Amy is still missing," Kraus told me.

"I'm sorry to hear that," I said.

Peak abruptly turned from the photograph. "Interested in anatomy, is he?" he asked.

"Anatomy?"

"It looks like a science project," Peak said. "In the picture here. Organs?"

"Yes."

"So, he's interested in that, your son?"

I shook my head. "Not really, no."

Kraus's smile was thin, anemic, forced rather than felt. "So why did he do a project like that?" he asked

"Because it was easy for him," I answered.

"Easy?"

"Other kids had much more elaborate projects," I explained.

"He's not a great student then?"

"No."

"How would you describe him?" Kraus asked.

"Keith? I don't know. He's a teenage boy. A little odd, maybe."

"In what way is he odd?"

"Well, not odd exactly," I added quickly. "Quiet."

Kraus looked at Peak and gave a faint nod, which brought the smaller man suddenly back into the game.

"No reason to be alarmed," Peak said.

"I'm not alarmed," I told him.

The two men exchanged glances.

"I suppose you'd like to talk to Keith," I added, careful to keep my voice firm and confident, a father who has not the slightest doubt that he knows his son thoroughly. I wanted them to believe that nothing could have escaped my notice—that I had searched Keith's closets and the drawers of his bedroom bureau, smelled his breath when he came in at night, routinely dragged him to the family physician for drug tests; that I monitored the books he read, the music he listened to, the sites he visited on the Internet; that I had researched the family histories of the friends he hung around with; that only God could possibly know more than I did about my son.

"Yes, we would," Kraus said.

"I'll get him."

"He's not here," Meredith said quickly.

I looked at her, puzzled. "Where is he?"

"He went for a walk."

Before I could say anything further, Kraus said, "Where does he walk?"

For some reason, Meredith merely repeated the question. "Where does he walk?"

Peak looked out the large window that fronted the thickly forested grounds behind the house. "Back there, that's conservation land, right? No houses. No roads."

"Yes, it's all conservation land," I told him. "No one can ever build back there or—"

"So it's very isolated," Peak said. He turned back to Meredith. "Is that where Keith takes these walks, in the woods back there?"

Suddenly the words "these walks" took on an ominous quality and I imagined Keith as I knew Peak and Kraus imagined him, a figure crouching in the undergrowth, desperately digging in the moist ground, burying something that linked him to Amy Giordano, a bloodstained lock of hair.

"No, he doesn't walk back there," I said quickly. "You can't. The undergrowth is too thick and there are no trails."

Kraus's eyes shifted to my wife, fixing on her an unsettling intensity. "So where is he?"

"The baseball field," Meredith answered. "When he goes for a walk, he usually goes down to the baseball field."

"There and back, you mean?" Peak asked.

Meredith nodded faintly, and I expected that to be the end of it, but Kraus said, "When does he go for these walks? In the morning?"

"No," Meredith answered. "Usually in the afternoon. Or after dinner."

"Not in the morning then," Kraus said. "Except this morning, right?"

Again, Meredith nodded delicately, like someone reluctant to give assent, but unable to withhold it.

"I noticed a bike at the end of the walkway," Peak said. "Is that Keith's?"

"Yes," I said. "He uses it to make deliveries for me after school."

"Where does he make these deliveries?" Kraus asked.

"Anywhere in biking distance from my shop," I said.

"And that would be where, Mr. Moore?" Peak asked.

"My shop is in Dalton Square," I said.

"What does he deliver?" Kraus asked.

"Pictures," I said. "Of families, mostly."

"Family photographs," Peak said with a slight smile. "Got a few of those myself."

Kraus shifted his weight like a fighter preparing to deliver the next blow. "How long has he been delivering these pictures?"

Again, there was a sinister, oddly accusatory, use of "these," but I was no longer sure if the accusation was intended to incriminate Keith or if Kraus had now extended his accusatory tone to me.

"A couple of years," I answered. "There's no law against that, is there?"

"What?" Peak asked with a slight chuckle. "Well, of course not, Mr. Moore." He glanced toward Kraus then back to me. "Why would you think that?"

Before I could answer, Meredith cut in. "I'll go get him if you want me to."

Peak looked at his watch. "No, we'll do it. The ball field's on the way back to the station, we can—"

"No!" I blurted. "Let me bring him here."

Both of them looked at me, stonily silent, waiting.

"It would scare him," I explained.

"What would scare him?" Kraus asked.

"You know, two men he's never seen."

"He's a scared type of kid, your son?" Peak asked.

It had never occurred to me before, but now it struck me that in fact Keith was a "scared type of kid." He was scared he'd disappointed Meredith by doing poorly in school and scared he'd disappointed me by never having had a girlfriend. He was scared he wouldn't get into a good college, scared that he'd never find what he wanted to do in life or that he'd fail at the thing he did find. He had no friends, and I supposed that that scared him, too. Add them up, one by one, and it seemed that he was scared of almost everything, lived in a subtle crouch. And yet, I said, "No, I don't think Keith's scared of anything in particular. But two men—police—that would scare anybody, wouldn't it?"

Again, Kraus and Peak glanced at each other, then Peak said. "All right, Mr. Moore, you can go get him." He regarded me distantly. "No reason," he repeated, "to be alarmed."

I expected to find Keith on Vernon Road, which fronts our house, then shoots directly to town, where it becomes Main Street, then winds another mile to the ball field, a distance of little more than three miles. But instead, I spotted him standing idly at the little playground near the town square, a place where people routinely bring small children to scrabble in the sandbox or race around the wooden castle. He was slumped against the playground's wrought iron fence, his shoulder pressed into it, rhythmically kicking at the ground with the toe of his shoe.

He didn't see me when I pulled up to the curb a few yards from the playground, so that by the time I'd gotten out of the car and walked across the lawn, it was too late for him to hide the cigarette.

"I didn't know you smoked," I said, as I came up to him.

He whirled around, clearly startled, his gaze first on me, then darting nervously about the grounds, as if in fear of snipers.

I nodded toward the pack of Marlboros that winked from his shirt pocket. "When did you start?"

He took a long, defiant draw on the cigarette, his body now assuming a sullen teenage swagger. "I don't do it all the time."

"So, in this case, what's the occasion?"

He shrugged. "I guess I'm jumpy." He let the cigarette drop from his fingers, lifted the collar of his parka, and in that instant he seemed to retreat to an earlier time, taking on the sullen hunch of a fifties teenager, a rebel without a cause.

"This thing with Amy," I said. "It makes everybody jumpy."

"Yeah, sure." He ground the cigarette into the dirt with the toe of his shoe, snatched the pack from his shirt pocket, thumped out another and lit it.

"It's okay to be a little nervous," I told him.

He waved out the match and laughed. "Oh yeah?"

"I would be," I said.

"But there's a difference, Dad." He took a long draw on the cigarette and released a column of smoke that narrowly missed my face. "You weren't at her fucking house."

He'd never used that kind of language in front of me before, but it didn't seem the right time to quibble about matters that now struck me as infinitely small. The last thing he needed, I decided, was a scolding.

"I have to take you back home," I told him.

This appeared to disturb him more than my having caught him with a cigarette.

"I want to hang around here for a while," he said.

"No, you have to come with me," I insisted. "There are a couple of policemen who want to talk to you."

His face stiffened and an icy fear came into his eyes. "They think I did it, right?"

"Did what?"

"You know, whatever happened to Amy."

"There's no evidence that anything happened to Amy."

"Yeah, but something did," Keith said. "Something did, or she wouldn't be missing."

"Keith," I said. "I want you to be very careful when you talk to these cops. Think before you answer. And be sure you don't lie about anything."

"Why would I lie about something?" Keith asked.

"Just don't, that's what I'm telling you. Because it's a red flag."

He dropped the cigarette and crushed it with an odd brutality, as if he were angrily stomping the life out of a small defenseless creature. "I didn't hurt Amy."

"I know that."

"I may be bad, but I didn't hurt Amy."

"You're not bad, Keith. Smoking cigarettes doesn't make you bad."

A dry scoffing laugh broke from him, one whose exact meaning I couldn't read. "Yeah, right, Dad" was all he said.

Meredith had served Kraus and Peak coffee and cookies by the time I returned with Keith, but I couldn't imagine that she'd been able to do it in a way that actually made them feel welcome.

"This is Keith," I told them as I ushered my son into the living room.

Both detectives rose and smiled and shook Keith's hand. Then they sat down on the green sofa, Keith opposite them in a wooden rocker.

"You don't have to stay," Peak said to Meredith. He looked at me. "You, either, Mr. Moore. This is just a friendly chat." He smiled. "If it were any more serious than that, we'd be reading Keith here his rights." He glanced at Keith and the smile broadened. "Just like they do on TV, right?"

Keith nodded slightly.

"I'd rather stay with my son," I said.

Meredith opted to busy herself in her small office at the rear of the house, however, and so it was just three men and a teenage boy in the living room when the questioning began.

Then, almost immediately, it was over, with little more established than what I'd already told Vince Giordano, that Keith had not left Amy alone in her house, that he'd gotten home a little before midnight. The only new facts were that my son had walked from Amy's house into the village, then along its back streets, and finally over to the ball field where he'd sat alone on the bleachers for a time, then gotten up and walked home. At no time during this late-night sojourn had he talked to anyone. He'd called home at just before ten, he said. I'd answered the phone and he'd told me that he intended to stay out a little later than usual. I'd asked if he needed a ride, and he'd assured me that he didn't. At that point, he and I had agreed that he was to be home before midnight. Which, he told Kraus and Peak, he had been. The exact time, he said, was seven minutes before twelve. He knew this because he'd glanced at the large grandfather clock in the front foyer before going upstairs to his room.

As I listened to Keith's answers, I began to relax. Nothing Keith said surprised me and nothing contradicted my own understanding of his movements and activities that night.

"So," Kraus said, "after you hung around the ball field for a while, you went straight home?"

"Yes."

"The ball field is only a few blocks from the Giordanos' house, isn't it?"

"Yes."

"Did you pass their house again?"

"No."

"You went straight home," Peak said, "Like DO NOT PASS GO?"

Keith chuckled, but mirthlessly, a laugh I heard as a mocking response to Peak's reference.

And so it didn't surprise me that Peak's attitude immediately hardened. "How'd you get home?"

"I walked."

Peak's eyes were very still. "You walked?"

"Yes," Keith answered.

"You don't have a car?" Kraus asked.

"No," Keith said. "I couldn't drive anyway. I'm fifteen."

"You have a learner's permit?" Peak asked.

"Yes."

"How did you get to Amy's house?"

"My uncle drove me."

Kraus took a notebook from his jacket pocket. "What's your uncle's name?"

Keith looked at me as if asking if he should answer.

"His name is Warren," I said. "Warren Moore."

"Where does he live?" Kraus asked.

"1473 Barrow Street."

"Near the school," Peak said. "The elementary school."

"Yes," I said. "Right next door, actually."

"Where does he work?"

"He works on his own. He paints houses."

Kraus jotted something in his notebook, then returned his attention to Keith. "So your uncle drove you to Amy's house, and then, after Mr. and Mrs. Giordano came back home, you walked to town—have I got that right?"

"Yes."

"And then you went to the ballfield, and after that you walked home?"

"Yes."

"All the way from the center of town?"

Keith nodded.

"You didn't get a ride?" Kraus asked.

Keith shook his head. "No."

"But you could have called home, right, gotten a lift?"

"Sure."

"Why didn't you?" Peak asked.

"I just didn't," Keith answered. "I don't mind walking."

"Even that late?" Kraus asked.

"No," Keith answered. He thrust his head backward and ran his fingers through the tangles of his hair. "I like the night," he said.

SIX

I *like the night.*

Odd how sinister a simple remark can sound, the questions it can suddenly raise.

In what way, I wondered, did my son like the night? Did he like it because it brought him a certain peace? Or did he like it simply because it meant the end of another tedious day at school or at home? Or did he like it because it shielded him from view, because, clothed in its darkness, he could skulk about unnoticed, hidden beneath the hood of the blue parka? Did he like it like a saint in search of solitude or like a stalker in search of cover?

It didn't matter really. What mattered was that my son had gotten through it, so that it might end here, a hope I fully embraced as I walked the two detectives to their car.

Kraus got in behind the wheel, but Peak remained standing at the passenger door. He wore a dark green suit, and in the slant of bright sunlight that washed over him, he looked like a thick shrub.

"Mr. Moore," he said, "what is your experience with your son?"

"Experience?" I asked.

"In your exchanges, I mean. Day to day."

"I still don't quite . . ."

"Has he been truthful?" Peak asked.

Suddenly, I thought of the two beams of light sweeping across the ragged undergrowth and recalled that only moments before, Keith had said that he had not been driven home the night before. *Was that true?* I wondered now. But despite that jarring vision and its accompanying doubt, I said, "As far as I know, he's always told me the truth."

Peak watched me closely. "About everything?"

"Well, I'm sure he's told a few little lies to me over the years," I said. "He's a kid, that's all. A little enclosed, but—" The look in Peak's eyes stopped me in my tracks. "But normal," I added quickly. "A teenager, that's all."

"Yes, of course," Peak said.

He tried to appear perfectly satisfied by my answer, but I knew he wasn't. "Well, thank you," he said. "We'll call if we need anything further."

With that he settled into the passenger seat and the car pulled away.

Meredith was washing the detectives' coffee cups when I returned to the house, her movements strangely frantic, almost violent, like someone trying to erase an incriminating stain.

"Well, that was easier than I expected," I told her.

"They'll be back," Meredith said.

Her certainty surprised me. "Why are you so sure of that?"

She had been facing the sink, her back to me, but now she whirled around. "Because something always comes up, Eric." There was a fire in her eyes, a sense that she was talking about more than Keith's connection, whatever it might be, to Amy Giordano's disappearance.

"What do you mean?"

"To spoil things"—her expression took on an indecipherable combination of anger and sadness, like someone mourning a death by freak accident—"when things were so perfect."

"Nothing is spoiled," I said in a gentle, comforting tone, pleased that our life had seemed so perfect to her until now. "Meredith, we don't even know what happened to Amy yet."

She glanced away, settled her gaze briefly on the woods outside the window, two small birds in a hanging feeder. "I just feel this terrible sinking," she said softly.

I came over to her and drew her into my arms. Her body was stiff and brittle, a bundle of sticks. "Nothing is sinking," I assured her.

She shook her head. "I'm just afraid, that's all. Afraid that it's all going to . . . explode."

With that, she stepped out of my embrace and made her way up the stairs. I made no effort to follow her. It wouldn't have done any good anyway. Under stress, Meredith preferred being alone, at least in brief intervals. There was something about solitude that calmed her, and so I left her to herself, walked out into the yard, sat beside the brick grill, and tried to reason through my impulsive decision to say nothing to the police or even to Keith about my oddly building suspicion that he'd lied to them. Even then, I wasn't sure why I'd done it, save that I'd found no way to address the matter without either drawing Keith deeper into suspicion or grilling him myself, an action I wanted to delay as long as possible in the hope that Amy would suddenly turn up safe and sound, and so there would be no need for me to confront Keith at all. It was an illusion that couldn't be justified, or even maintained for very long, and I should have known that at the time. Since then I've learned that half of life is denial, that even in those we love, it's not what we see but what we choose to be blind to that sustains us.

I was still sitting in the same place when Warren's car made the lazy turn around the driveway and came to a halt in front of the house.

He got out and headed toward me, his gait far more determined than I'd ever seen it, an awkwardly charging bull.

"I just heard it on the radio," he said breathlessly when he reached me. "They're organizing a search. Volunteers. The whole town is gearing up for it." His face was red and appeared a bit puffy, the way it looked after he'd been drinking.

"So," he asked. "Are you okay?"

"I just hope Amy turns up," I said. "Because if she doesn't—"

"Don't think about that," Warren blurted.

This piece of advice did not surprise me. It was precisely

the advice Warren had spent his life following. I recalled how he'd put my father's bankruptcy out of his mind, pretending that our precipitous fall into poverty had simply never happened. And so he'd obliviously urged me to hold to my plan to go to college, though there was no money for that. Years later, with my father now in a low-rent retirement home, he'd broached the subject of our starting a landscaping business. When I'd asked how he intended to come up with sufficient seed money, he'd replied, "Well, you know, when Pop goes," even though our father had long ago lost everything he had, everything he might have given us. Warren had reacted to Jenny's illness the same way, by simply refusing to face it. During the months of her dying, as she grew steadily weaker, losing one faculty after another to the growing tumor in her brain, Warren had talked on and on about a future she could not possibly have. "When Jenny gets a boyfriend," he'd say, or "When Jenny gets to high school." Only once, the afternoon of Jenny's death, when she lay mute and helpless, but nonetheless frantically trying to communicate, had he actually looked stricken by her circumstances. In my mind I could still see the way he'd stood at the door as she squirmed and sputtered, unable to speak, but seized with a raw determination to make some final statement. I'd leaned down and put my ear to her lips, heard nothing but her feverish breathing until even that had ended and she sank into a coma from which she never awakened.

Now Warren was with me once again in a time of trial, and once again he was refusing to admit the nature of the problem or how grave it might be or yet become.

"So," Warren said, "I just wanted to tell you that it's going to be okay, Bro."

There was no point in arguing with him, so I said simply, "The police have already been here. Keith told them that he never left Amy's house and that he walked home alone."

Warren plopped into a lawn chair opposite the grill and folded his hands over his belly. "The police had to talk to him," he said. "But they wouldn't think he had anything to do with something bad."

There it was again, mindless optimism, my brother's particular form of adaptation. He'd found a way to survive by taking in only the information that kept him afloat. In high school, he'd played the happy fat boy. In adulthood, the role of jovial alcoholic had fit like a glove. Now he was playing the steady family adviser, a role that clearly pleased him until I said, "They'll probably talk to you, too."

Warren smiled, but with a hint of nervousness. "Me? Why would they talk to me? I'm not involved."

"Of course you are, Warren."

The faint smile now drooped. "How?"

"You drove Keith to Amy's house," I explained.

"So?"

"I'm just telling you that they know about it," I said. "They asked for your address. They have to talk to everybody, Warren. Anyone who had any contact with Amy in the hours before she disappeared."

Warren said nothing, but his mind was clearly working hard.

"Did you have any contact with her?" I asked evenly.

"I wouldn't call it . . . contact."

"Did you see her?"

Warren didn't answer, but I knew from the look in his eyes that he had.

"Where was she?" I asked.

Warren's face grew very still. "She was in the yard when I let Keith out in front of the house. Playing. She came up to the car."

I leaned forward. "Listen to me," I said. "This is serious business. So I'll tell you what I told Keith. When the cops come to you, when they ask you questions, think before you answer. And tell the truth."

Warren nodded gently, obediently, like a child receiving grave instructions.

"Did you talk to Amy?" I asked.

Warren shook his head.

"Not even a quick hi?"

"I don't know," Warren said.

"Think, Warren."

He shrugged. "Maybe something like that, like what you said. You know, a quick hi."

"Nothing else?"

"No."

"Are you sure?"

"Yes," Warren answered.

I could see that he was worried now, but I also knew that this worry wouldn't last, his momentary fretfulness precisely that—momentary. Or so I thought. But to my surprise the veil of trouble didn't lift from my brother's face.

"Do you think they suspect me?" he asked.

"Why would they suspect you?"

Warren shrugged. "I don't know," he said weakly. "Maybe they just do."

I shook my head. "They have no reason to suspect you, Warren," I assured him.

But the pained expression remained on his face, an expression that reminded me of the look on Meredith's face, and on Keith's, so that it seemed to me that trouble had fallen upon my family like a net, leaving all our faces webbed in gray. "Everybody's a little worried at the moment"—I placed my hand on his shoulder and gave it a brotherly squeeze—"but it's nothing," I said, "compared to what Vince and Karen must be going through. A missing daughter, can you imagine?"

Warren nodded. "Yeah," he said quietly. "Such an adorable little girl."

SEVEN

Here is the illusion—a normal day predicts a normal to-morrow and each day is not a brand-new spin of the wheel, our lives not lived at the whim of Lady Luck. And yet, now, when I recall the morning in question, a bright sunny morning, before that first ring of the phone, I see myself as living in a world that was almost entirely illusion. Then the phone rang and I heard Vince Giordano's voice, and suddenly the wheel stopped. Instead of falling on the number upon which I'd bet the full wealth and value of my life and which it had always landed on before, the red ball skirted past, made another circle around the wheel, and dropped into a very dif-ferent slot. And like a gambler who'd won every spin before that moment, I stared, dazed, at the grim result of this latest turn of the wheel, and in my mind I set the wheel going back-ward, lifted the ball from the fateful slot, and sent it whirling back as if by sheer force of will it could be made to fall again where it had fallen so many times before. It was the afternoon of the day that Amy Giordano disappeared, but I refused to accept the fact that anything had changed.

And so, when I returned to the shop, I tried to appear normal, as if nothing were bothering me.

But Neil knew better. He attempted to hide it, but I often caught him glancing at me surreptitiously, as if I'd begun to manifest some curious symptom, a slight tremor in the hand, for example, or a peculiar tendency to stare into space.

"Something wrong, boss?" he asked finally.

By then the local radio stations had been reporting Amy's disappearance for several hours. People were searching her neighborhood, as well as more remote areas, particularly the woods that surrounded the subdivision where she lived. It was a big story, and so I knew that it was only a matter of time before the whole community would find out that Keith had been babysitting Amy the night of her disappearance.

"It's about Amy Giordano," I said. "Keith was at her house last night. Babysitting. The police spoke to him this morning."

The layer of jovial self mockery with which Neil presented himself dropped away. "I'm sure Keith didn't do anything wrong," he said. "Keith's very responsible."

Keith was no such thing, and I knew it. Although he was supposed to come to the shop immediately after school each afternoon, he often showed up an hour late, usually with a grudging look on his face, wanting only to go directly home, then just as directly up the stairs to his room. If there were deliveries to be made, he would make them, but always sullenly. He was not responsible in his schoolwork or in his chores at home. When he raked leaves, he usually did little more than scatter them. When he took out the garbage, a few pieces always failed to make it into the can. There was something desultory in everything he did, and for the first time, this very desultoriness took on an oddly sinister character, an outward carelessness and indifference to order that struck me as perhaps emblematic of an inner, and far more serious, disarray.

Neil touched my arm. "You don't have to worry about Keith," he said. "He's a good kid."

It was typical of Neil to say whatever had to be said to ease my distress, and the only response I could think of was a quick, false "Yes, he is."

Neil smiled warmly, then returned to his work, though I noticed that each time the phone rang he tensed and glanced over at me worriedly.

Until just before two that afternoon, all the calls were routine, and during those few hours I felt the sweetness of the ordinary, of needs easily met, promises easily kept, a world of choices and decisions that demanded no great store of wisdom.

At 1:54 the phone rang.

It was Detective Peak. "Mr. Moore, I wanted to let you know that—"

"You found her," I blurted.

"What?" Peak asked.

"You found Amy," I repeated.

"No," he said. "I wish we had. I'm just calling because I

need your assurance that Keith will be around if we need to talk to him again."

"Of course, he will."

"This is an official request, Mr. Moore," Peak said. "Keith is now in your custody."

Custody. The word was abruptly laden with grave responsibility.

"He won't go anywhere," I told him.

"Good," Peak said. "Thank you for your cooperation."

He hung up, but for a brief instant, I continued to press the receiver to my ear, hoping for another voice to come on the line, to tell me that Amy had been found, that she was alive and well, just a little girl who'd wandered out of her house, crawled into a storm drain, and gone to sleep.

"Boss?"

It was Neil. He was staring at me from behind a counter piled with small boxes of film.

"It was the police," I told him. "They want to make sure Keith doesn't go anywhere."

Neil's lips parted, but he didn't speak.

I put down the phone. "I think I should probably go home, Neil."

"Sure," Neil said. "I'll lock up if you . . ."

"Thanks."

I walked to my car and got in, but didn't start the engine. Instead I sat, nearly motionless behind the wheel, watching people on the sidewalk, some alone, a few couples, a scattering of families with children. They strolled past the little shops with an air of complete casualness, like swimmers in the sea, untroubled, caught in that carefree instant before the dark fin breaks the surface and sends them thrashing toward shore.

Before I started home I snapped up my cell phone and called Meredith.

"Peak called me," I told her. "We have to keep an eye on Keith."

She could tell by the tone of my voice that I was feeling shaky. "That means they suspect him," she said.

"I'm not sure you can draw that conclusion."

"Oh please, Eric," Meredith said, her tone faintly irritated. "You can't live with your head in the sand forever. We have to face things."

"I'm facing them, it's just that—"

"Where are you now?" she interrupted.

"I'm just leaving the shop."

"Good. We need to talk."

She was waiting in the living room when I arrived.

"It's all that's on the radio," she said. "A big story for this shitty little town."

I had never heard her speak of Wesley in such a hateful way, as if she felt trapped by its smallness, ensnared and suffocating. Had she felt this way for a long time? I wondered. Had she sometimes awakened in the night and wanted to rush to the family car and drive away, out of Wesley, toward some bright horizon she'd never spoken of? In movies, people always had secret dreams, and I'd assumed that at least a few real people actually had them, but I'd never thought Meredith afflicted by such dreaminess. Now I wondered if she harbored some thwarted fantasy, dreamed of yellow-brick roads and princely palaces, of being king of some hill she'd never had a chance to climb.

She walked over to the sofa and sat down hard, as if she were trying to squash the world beneath her. "They mentioned that Vince and Karen had gone out for the evening but not that there was a babysitter"—she shook her head—"but that'll come," she said crisply. "There had to have been a babysitter. Amy was eight years old."

"Was?" I asked darkly.

"You know what I mean." She looked at me determinedly. "I think we should call Leo."

I don't know why I resisted, except that some part of me was determined to keep the gravest consequences at bay, a hope, foolishly held, that if I simply refused to take the next step then no one else would take it, either.

"Not yet," I said.

"Why?" Meredith demanded.

"Because it'll make Keith look guilty," I answered. "You've seen how they do it on television. They say, 'So-and-so has retained counsel.' And people think, Okay the guy knows he did it and so now he's trying to protect himself."

Meredith stood up, walked to the back window, and peered out into the woods. "I hope you're right, Eric," she said.

I let her cool a moment, then said, "Do you think we should call the Giordanos?"

She shrugged.

"I think it would be a good idea," I said. "You know, to show our concern."

I walked into the kitchen, took the phone, and dialed the number.

A strange voice answered, but one I recognized. It was Detective Kraus. I told him who I was and that I wanted to express my hope that Amy would be returned safely home and offer my help, my family's help, in finding her. I asked to speak to Vince. Kraus said he'd get him. I heard him put the phone down, then his footsteps as he walked across the room. I could hear voices, but they were low and distant. Then the footsteps returned.

"Mr. Giordano doesn't want to talk," Kraus said. "He's a little . . . well . . . upset."

"Of course," I said.

"Keith's around, right?" Kraus asked.

"Yes."

"Because we have a few more questions for him."

I told him that Keith would be more than willing to help in any way he could, then put down the phone. Meredith was watching me worriedly.

"Maybe you're right," I told her. "Maybe we should call Leo."

Leo agreed to come over immediately, and so I went upstairs to talk to Keith.

The door to his room was closed and locked, as he'd insisted upon from the time he was thirteen. I'd never thought anything unusual about this. Teenagers were like that. They shut their parents out. It was a matter of asserting their independence, I supposed, part of the ritual of growing up and growing away. But now the fact that my son spent so much time in his room, at his computer, alone, behind a locked door, gave off an air of something hidden. What, I wondered, did he do in there? And in his solitude, what thoughts came to him?

I knocked at the door. "Keith."

I heard a strange scrambling, as if he were taken unawares and was now readying the room before opening the door, turning off the computer, closing drawers, perhaps quickly secreting things in his closet or beneath his bed.

I tapped again, this time more urgently. "Keith?"

The bolt snapped back, then the door opened to its customary two inches, and the single blue eye appeared.

"We've called a lawyer," I said.

The blue eye gave nothing away.

"Leo Brock," I added. "He's coming over in a few minutes."

The blue eye stared at me without sparkle, a tiny pool of unmoving water.

"I need to talk to you before he gets here."

Keith's voice was emotionless. "What about?"

I looked at the slowly blinking eye and wondered if Keith had taken something, inhaled something, if this, too, was a part of him he had hidden from me.

"Open the door," I said.

The door remained in place.

"What do we need to talk about?" Keith asked.

"Keith, open the door," I insisted.

He hesitated briefly, then drew back the door, but instead of ushering me into his room, he came out into the corridor and quickly closed the door behind him.

"Okay," he said. "Talk."

I looked at him closely. "Are you okay?"

He laughed softly, almost mockingly. "Yeah, great," he said.

"I mean are you . . . able to talk?"

He shrugged comically and grinned at me, but it was a cold grin, like a bitter clown. "What do you want, Dad?"

"I want you to tell the truth, Keith," I said. "When Mr. Brock comes over here. Whatever he asks you, tell him the truth."

"Like with the cops," Keith said.

"Like I told you to do, yes."

Again, he shrugged. "Okay . . . so?"

"The truth," I repeated, this time sternly.

"The truth, right," Keith said. His eyes narrowed slightly. "Is there something else?"

"In every detail," I said. "What you did while you were at Amy's. Where you went after that. How you got home. The truth, Keith."

"Yeah, okay." He waved his hand, as if batting away a pesky insect. "Can I go back now?"

I told him that he could, then watched as he slunk back behind the door and returned the bolt to its place, sealing himself off again.

Downstairs, Meredith was sitting at the kitchen table,

drinking coffee, her long fingers fidgeting nervously with the top button of her blouse.

"What did he say?" she asked.

"Nothing."

She took a sip from the cup. "Typical."

"What do you mean by that?"

"It's the same way he acted when we told him Amy was missing. No real reaction. A shrug. Like it was nothing."

"He didn't know how to react," I said.

Meredith didn't buy it. "I don't know, Eric, there should have been some little expression of sympathy . . . shock . . . something." She took another sip of coffee. "He didn't ask a single question. Did you notice that?"

"He's afraid," I told her.

She drew in a quick agitated breath. "So am I," she said.

I could see that clearly, her fear, and in that first visible dread, felt the touch of something yet more dreadful still.

"Are you all right?" I asked.

"How could I be all right, Eric?" Meredith asked. Her voice was edged in sarcasm. "How can anything be all right?" She took an angry sip from the cup, grim, resigned, though I couldn't tell if this resignation had to do with Keith or me or herself, or just the life that was hers, the whole course by which she'd come to rest in a shitty little town.

I had no answer for her, and so I did what we often do when things seem beyond us, wrapped in total darkness, when we sense the approaching precipice.

I reached out blindly and took her hand.

EIGHT

Leo preferred to meet Keith at our house rather than at his office because, as he told Meredith, "Kids are less jumpy on their home turf."

We'd known Leo for nearly fifteen years. When the time had come to buy the shop, I'd picked his name out of the local phone book, and he'd conducted the closing with such effortless competence that he'd handled all our personal and business affairs ever since. More recently, he'd also become something of a family friend. His wife, Peg, had died three years before, and since then Meredith had made a few attempts to match him up with various faculty members at the community college. Leo had never once called any of these women, however, and Meredith had finally gotten the message that he simply did not want to marry again. He was happy as a sixty-two-year-old widower, free to do as he pleased, take off on a whim.

He arrived at precisely 3:15, dressed in his customary jacket and tie, his shoes polished to a gleaming sheen.

"Hello, Eric," he said when I opened the door.

I led him into the living room, where Meredith sat at the end of the sofa, her long legs primly crossed, hands in her lap, a rigid posture Leo noticed immediately.

"I know this is very disturbing," he told her as he sat down on the sofa. "But, believe me, it's much too early to suggest that Keith has anything at all to worry about." He glanced around the room. "Speaking of which, where is he?"

"In his room," I said. "I thought you might want to talk to us first."

Leo shook his head. "No, Keith is actually the person I need to talk with."

It was a clear instruction to summon Keith downstairs.

"I'll get him," Meredith said. She rose and headed up the stairs.

"This is all very strange," I said after she'd left the room. "Keith involved in something like this."

"Naturally, it's worrisome," Leo said. "But nine times out of ten, everything can be cleared up very quickly."

"You've handled this kind of thing before?" I asked.

Leo leaned back casually. "What kind of thing is that?"

"A kid accused of something," I answered.

"Has Keith been accused of anything?"

"Not exactly but . . ."

"But what?"

"Well, he was the last person to see Amy."

Leo shook his head. "No, the last person to see Amy was the guy who took her." He looked at me significantly. "You need to keep that distinction firmly in mind, Eric."

I nodded obediently.

Meredith returned, Keith dragging along behind her, looking tense, like someone already tried and found guilty who was now only awaiting the judge's sentence.

"Hi, Keith," Leo said brightly. He rose and thrust out his hand with the exuberance of a patriot welcoming a soldier home. "You look like you're holding up just fine." He glanced at me, then offered Keith a wink. "Not like your old man, huh?"

Keith smiled, but it was a smile I'd seen before, mirthless and rather resentful, as if the whole thing were a dreadful inconvenience, something he had to go through before he could get back to his computer game.

"Have a seat," Leo said as he lowered himself back onto the sofa.

Keith sat down in the chair across the narrow coffee table. He looked at me, then back at Leo. In his eyes I saw nothing but a dull determination to endure the next few minutes, then slink back to the dark burrow of his room.

"So, I hear the cops came by," Leo began. His tone was light, almost chatty. He might have been asking Keith about a favorite movie. "They stay long?"

Keith shook his head.

"Good," Leo said. "They're not much fun to have around, are they?"

Again, Keith shook his head.

Leo flung one hand over the back of the sofa and with the other unbuttoned his jacket with a great show of casualness. "What'd they want to know?"

"About Amy," Keith said with a halfhearted shrug.

Leo's next question was carried on the back of a slight yawn. "What'd you tell them?"

"That I put her to bed at around eight-thirty."

"And that was the last time you saw her?"

"Yes."

"When did you leave Amy's house?"

"When her parents came home."

"And that would be?"

"Around ten."

Leo leaned forward with a soft grunt and leisurely massaged his ankle. "Then what?"

For the next few minutes, I listened as my son told Leo the same story he'd told the police—that he'd gone into the village, wandered the streets, lingered awhile at the ball field, then walked home. As he spoke, I let myself believe that he might actually be telling the truth, that perhaps I was wrong and hadn't really heard a car stop on the road that night, watched its lights sweep through the undergrowth, then draw away. I'd seen other parents find ways to deny the horrible possibility that their son or daughter might have done a terrible thing. In the past, the way they'd demonstrated such blind faith in their child's innocence had amazed me. But suddenly, when Leo turned to me and said, "Were you awake when Keith came home?" I knew that I was now one of those parents, willing to do or say or believe anything that would hold back the grim tide of doubt.

"Yes, I was awake," I answered.

"So you saw Keith when he came home?"

"Yes."

"When did you see him?"

"I heard him come down the driveway," I said.

Mercifully the next question—*Was he alone?*—never came, a blank I made no effort to fill in.

Leo smiled at me appreciatively. "Good," he said, as if I were a schoolboy who'd spelled the word correctly. He turned to Keith. "I'll keep track of the investigation for you." He leaned over and patted my son's knee. "Don't worry about a thing." He started to rise, then stopped and lowered himself back down on the sofa. "One other thing," he said, his eyes on Keith. "Were you ever over around the water tower?"

I saw a dark sparkle in my son's eyes.

"Water tower?" Keith asked.

"The town water tower, you know where it is, don't you?" Leo said. "About a mile outside town."

"I know where it is," Keith answered warily, as if it were a guilty knowledge.

"So, were you ever over that way?"

Keith shook his head. "No," he said.

With no further word, Leo got abruptly to his feet again. "Well, I'll keep you all informed as this thing goes forward," he said. He turned and walked to the door. "Well, have a nice day."

Meredith stepped forward quickly. "I'll walk you to your car, Leo," she said.

Seconds later I was alone in the living room, Keith upstairs, Meredith and Leo strolling down the walkway toward his impressive black Mercedes.

Briefly, I sat on the sofa, but anxiety soon overtook me, and I rose and walked to the front window. Meredith and Leo were standing beside his car, Leo nodding in that worldly way of his as he listened to Meredith. She seemed more animated than she'd been since Amy Giordano's disappearance, her hands fluttering about as if she were trying to catch an invisible butterfly. Then Leo said something, and her hands stopped their edgy flight, froze for a moment, and finally dropped to her sides like weights.

She listened as Leo spoke in what appeared to be slow, deliberate terms, her gaze fixed on him with great intensity until she abruptly glanced toward the house, the window where I stood, and in response to which, I stepped quickly out of view, like a peeper unexpectedly caught in the act.

I'd returned to the sofa by the time she came back into the house.

"Well, how do you think it went?" I asked.

She sat down beside me, calmer now, and less angry than before. "We'll get through this, won't we, Eric?" she asked.

"What?"

"No matter what happens, we'll get through it."

"Why wouldn't we?"

She appeared at a loss for an answer but said finally, "Because of the strain, the pressure. Sometimes families break."

"Or come together," I said. "Like those covered wagons when the Indians attack."

Her smile was ghostly faint. "Like covered wagons, yes," was all she said.

I went back to the shop a few minutes later, hoping that Leo Brock was right, that there was nothing to worry about.

"Everything okay?" Neil asked.

"Well, we have a lawyer now," I answered.

Neil received this in the way I'd offered it, as an indication that in some unknowable way things had grown more serious.

"If there's anything I can do," he said.

I'd always thought Neil a somewhat inconsequential man, not because he was clownishly gay and effeminate, but because he was so excessively emotional, easily moved by tear-jerker movies. But now that very excess struck me as sweet and genuine, an empathy that lay deep within him, like the marrow of his bones. And it struck me then that trouble was like a turn of a lens, a shift that brings everything into sharper focus. Suddenly, you see who cares and who doesn't, the genuinely kind and those who only fake their kindness.

"I just think that good people shouldn't, you know, have bad things happen to them," Neil added. "People like you and Meredith. Mr. and Mrs. Giordano. Innocent people. Like Amy."

"Yes."

"And Keith," Neil added.

Keith.

I felt a catch, as if a stream deep inside me, one that had always been open and freely flowing toward my son, had abruptly narrowed.

"Yes, Keith," I said.

Neil caught something in my eyes. "I just hope Keith has someone to talk to," he said, then edged away and pointedly busied himself with unpacking a box of camera cases.

I walked behind the framing counter and went to work. Several orders had come in during the previous afternoon. Neil had written them up on slips that gave the precise size and number of the frame required for each photograph. As usual, they were family pictures, save for one of a golden retriever as it loped along the shoreline. In one, a family was gathered on the steps of a small rented cottage, the father at the rear, tanned and shirtless, his arms draped over his wife's shoulders, two children seated on the wooden steps. In another, a much larger family was sprawled around a campsite, dappled sunlight falling through the overhanging limbs. Some were in bathing suits, and the teenage daughter's blond hair hung in wet curls as she dried it with a towel.

I read each slip, pulled the designated frame from stock, cut the glass, and leaned the completed work against the wall behind me. After that I wiped the counter and sat down on the short aluminum stool behind it.

I don't know how long I sat silently, waiting for the relief of an approaching customer, before I noticed the glossy edge of a photograph tucked just beneath the corner of the developing machine. It was crumpled badly, but when I placed it on the counter and smoothed it out, I saw that it was a picture of Amy Giordano. No doubt Neil had inadvertently dropped it on the floor some days before, one of the "free doubles" we gave out with each order.

In the photograph, she was standing alone at the edge of a glittering blue pool, clothed in a one-piece red and white polka-dot bathing suit. An enormous beach ball rested beside her, beads of water clinging to its soft plastic sides. A crinkle in the photograph sliced Amy's body diagonally in a cruel, jagged line, so that her raised right arm appeared severed from her body, as did her left leg at midcalf. Other than this accidental bisection, there was no suggestion of Amy's fate, and yet I felt a sudden, terrible presentiment that she had been murdered, and in that instant, without in the least willing it, I saw Keith standing at the end of an imagined corridor that led to Amy's room, his hands closed in tight fists, fighting the impulse that raged within him, trying desperately to control himself, the urge so fierce that he felt it as a hand shoving him from behind, heard it as a voice shouting madly inside his head, the force growing ever more furious until he finally gave way before it, fixed his eyes upon the closed door at the far end of the shadowy hallway, drew in a long breath, and began to move toward it.

"Eric?"

I blinked quickly and glanced toward the voice, half expecting to find a demon standing there, horned and red-eyed, incarnate evil. But it was only Mrs. Phelps, holding two rolls of film in a slightly tremulous hand. "I hope I can have this by

Tuesday," she said as she placed an eight-by-ten photo of her granddaughter on the counter before me. "Isn't she lovely?" she asked.

I quickly pocketed the photograph of Amy and concentrated instead on the other little girl. "Yes," I said, "she is."

I closed the shop at the usual time, and headed back home. Meredith was just hanging up the phone when I came into the kitchen.

"I was talking to Dr. Mays," she said. "He's having a cocktail party next weekend. We're invited. Do you want to go? I think we should."

"Why?"

"So we look . . . normal," Meredith said.

"We are normal, Meredith."

"You know what I mean."

"Yeah, okay," I said. "You're right. We can't let people think we have something to hide."

She nodded. "Especially now."

"Now? What do you mean?"

"Now that we know why Leo asked Keith if he'd ever been to the water tower."

"What are you talking about?"

"They found Amy's pajamas there," Meredith said. She looked at me quizzically. "Haven't you been listening to the radio?"

I shook my head. "No, I guess I prefer to avoid things."

To my surprise she said, "Yes, you do. Keith's the same way."

"What do you mean?"

"You're not confrontational, Eric. You're passive. So is he."

"What does that mean, exactly?"

"It means what it says. That you don't confront things."

"Like what?"

"Jesus, Eric, where should I begin? Like Keith's grades, for one thing. I'm the one who makes demands. And the way he just slouches around the house. I'm the one who gets on his back, makes him take out the garbage, rake the leaves."

This was true. There was no denying it.

"And it's not that you don't think that he should do these things," Meredith added. "It's just that you don't want to confront him. That's the way you are, passive."

I shrugged. "Maybe so. I don't feel like arguing about it."

"My point exactly," Meredith said crisply.

Her tone struck me as unnecessarily harsh. "Well, what had you rather me do, argue with him all the time? Argue with you? Make a big deal out of everything?"

"But some things are big deals," Meredith shot back. "Like whether your son is fucked-up or not. That's a big deal."

"Fucked-up?"

"Yes."

"How is Keith fucked-up?"

Meredith wagged her head in frustration. "Jesus, Eric. Don't you see anything?"

"I see a teenage boy. What's so fucked-up about him?"

"He has no friends, for God's sake," Meredith said emphatically. "Lousy grades. No sense of direction. Have you ever seen a spark of interest in anything, the slightest sign of ambition?" She looked oddly defeated. "When he graduates from high school, he'll work for you in the shop, that's what he'll do. He'll deliver pictures the way he does now, except that he'll use a car instead of a bicycle. Eventually, he'll take over Neil's job. And when you die, he'll take the shop over completely." She made no effort to conceal her disappointment in such a course. "That will be his life, Eric, a little frame and photo shop."

"Like my life?" I asked. "The poor, pathetic bastard."

She saw that she had struck too deep. "I didn't mean it like that. You had nothing. Your father went bankrupt. You had to fend for yourself. But Keith has all the advantages. He could go to any school, follow any star."

I waved my hand and turned away. There was something in this I couldn't bear. "I'm going for a walk," I told her irritably.

"A walk?" Meredith asked. She looked at me quizzically. "At this time of day? Where?"

I never went for walks, but I knew I had to get away. It didn't matter where I went, only that I got out of the house, away from Meredith and the sense of failure and disappointment that wafted from her like an odor.

I turned and headed for the door. "The woods" was all I said.

In Frost's famous poem, they are lovely, dark, and deep, but the sun had not yet set on the woods that evening, and so every detail of the undergrowth was visible to me, save its function, which was to hide whatever lay beneath it.

There were no trails in the woods behind the house, no route through the bramble, so I made my way slowly, cautiously, pushing aside low-slung limbs and clinging vines.

I remember the things that came to mind as I walked: Amy's disappearance, Keith's interrogation, the trouble I feared might be ahead. But more than anything, when I think of that last lone walk, I consider not the bare facts I knew at the time, nor the problems I reasonably anticipated, but the darker currents I knew nothing of, nor could have imagined.

Now, so many years later, as I wait in the corner booth of a diner on a rainy autumn afternoon, I review the long course of my unknowing. Then the words return again, *I'll be back before the news,* and my body stiffens as if against a crushing blow, and I am once again in woods without a trail, and darkness is closing in, and there is no way to get back home.

PART II

B eyond the diner window, the streets are crowded. Families mostly, cameras hanging from their arms. You have served them by the thousands. They ask only the simplest questions. They pull out their little canisters of film and ask how much it will cost to have their pictures developed. You quote them a price and if they're satisfied with it, they ask when the pictures will be ready. You answer that question, too, and in most cases the deal is done. You walk to the developing machine, open the canister, take out the film, feed it into the machine, and wait. The rollers inside the machine turn, the chemicals disperse. The motor hums. The minutes pass. Then the pictures emerge, shiny, new. They fall into the tray like brightly colored leaves.

The years go by, old customers drop away and new ones appear. You wonder if one of these new ones will recognize you, remember what happened, and ask a different question. Then one Sunday morning the phone rings, and you realize that a past without a future is a corpse, and that for a long time you have been dead. You want to rise from the grave, wrench something good from all that darkness, and so you say yes and make the arrangements.

But what will you say, you ask yourself, what will you say when you confront it all again? You want to end with wisdom, but you must begin without it because you had none when it began. You lived in a small town, lived a tidy little life. What you've learned since then, you've learned in increments, a treasure collected one coin at a time. And so you must chart the journey carefully, measure the pace, offer what you have gathered, and hope it will be accepted.

But first you must think it through again, return to that last moment, then double back to the days preceding it, how it happened that in a few short days everything fell apart. Yes, you decide, that's the way to tell it.

The waitress has no suspicion. She has seen other men like you, alone on a Sunday morning, sitting in the back booth, with nothing but a mug of coffee.

And so you feel safe here. And why not? You could not bring them back to life, could not repair the damage, and so you decided to make the best of it. You thought of leaving Wesley, but you didn't. You stayed because you believed there was a reason to stay, and that, in the end, you would find that reason. But the years passed, and you had begun to believe that you would never find it. Then the phone rang, and suddenly the reason was clear. You realized that, if nothing else, you could give a few things back, draw them like dried bones from your own buried past.

And so you have come here, to this diner, in hope of doing that, offering the paltry gift of the few dark things you know.

NINE

Suspicion is an acid, that's one thing I know. Everything it touches it corrodes. It eats through the smooth, glistening surface of things and the mark it leaves is indelible. Late one night, I watched a rerun of one of the Alien movies. In one scene, the alien pukes up a liquid so corrosive it immediately eats through first one floor of the space station, then another and another. And I thought, it's like that, suspicion, it has nowhere to go but down through level after level of old trusts and long devotions. Its direction is always toward the bottom.

I knew that things had changed in my family, that Meredith had grown more volatile and Keith more defiant, but I wasn't aware of how much Amy Giordano's disappearance had affected other, seemingly neutral, people. She had been missing for three days by then, and there could be no doubt that everyone in Wesley now knew that Keith had been Amy's

babysitter the night of her disappearance. Even so, I was to-
tally unprepared for Mrs. Phelps's reaction.

She was in her early seventies and had been a regular customer since the shop opened. She had white or bluish hair,
depending upon the competence of the beauty salon, and her
teeth were false and thus unnaturally even and a bit too large
for her mouth. She never came into the shop in anything but
dressy clothes, usually with a silk scarf around her neck, her
face fully made up down to the eye shadow.

She came into the store at just after ten. Neil was at the
front counter, and she stopped to chat with him in that amiable
way of hers. "Neil's very nice," she once said to me. But then, so
was almost everyone, according to Mrs. Phelps. Her gardener
was nice, for example, as was the Ecuadorian woman who
cleaned her house. Summer was nice, but so were spring and
fall. She'd never made particular mention of winter, but I had
no doubt she could find some aspect of it that was nice, too.

She had come to pick up the large photograph of her
granddaughter that she'd left for me to frame the preceding
weekend, and the minute she came through the door I remembered that it wasn't ready. I'd begun framing it before closing on Saturday, and Neil had quite correctly taken the frame
and photograph and placed them safely beneath the counter,
where they'd remained, completely forgotten until now.

"I'm sorry, Mrs. Phelps," I said when she walked up to the
counter. "I haven't finished the picture yet. I can have it for
you later today."

Mrs. Phelps smiled and waved her hand. "Oh, don't
worry, Eric," she said. "I'll come back for it later."

"No, no," I said. "It's my fault for not having it ready. When Keith gets here, I'll have him deliver it to you."

That's when I noticed an uneasy glimmer in Mrs. Phelps's eyes, a sudden, not very subtle wariness. I also knew the reason for it. Mrs. Phelps's granddaughter, the little girl in the photograph I had not yet framed, was staying with her. She was pretty, with long dark hair, and looked to be around eight years old, the same age and general appearance as Amy Giordano.

"Oh, you don't have to put Keith to that trouble," Mrs. Phelps said. "I'll drop by later this afternoon." Her voice remained kindly and accommodating, a nice woman being nice, but there was a firmness in it, too, a clear refusal to allow my son ever to come near her granddaughter. I thought of the whales I'd read about, how the mother whale will place her vast bulk between the harpoon and her offspring. Mrs. Phelps was doing no more than that, protecting her granddaughter from the dark potential of my son.

"All right," I said quietly. "If that's what you'd prefer."

"Yes, thank you," Mrs. Phelps said politely. She took a step backward, her gaze now fleeing to any available object, the smile still on her face, but lifeless, frozen. She was embarrassed by what she'd just done but unwilling to take it back. After all, she must have thought, her granddaughter's safety was at stake.

"Around four then," I said.

Mrs. Phelps nodded, turned, and walked rather hurriedly toward the door. She swept by Neil without nodding goodbye, and by the time she made it to the sidewalk I had the feeling that she was very nearly out of breath.

"Jesus," Neil said to me. "That was weird."

I stared out the front window, watching as Mrs. Phelps walked to her car and got in. "I don't think Keith should make deliveries anymore," I said.

"It's just awful," Neil said. "Whatever happened to innocent until proven guilty? And Mrs. Phelps, of all people. So nice, and all that, but . . ."

"It's fear," I told him, though until that moment I hadn't realized to what degree suspicion was a form of fear. "She's afraid of Keith. It's natural, I guess."

"But there's no reason for her to be afraid of Keith," Neil said.

I recalled the terrible vision I'd had a few days before, Keith moving down the shadowy corridor toward Amy's room. It was all I could do to keep from blurting the thought that came to me at that moment, *Dear God, I hope you're right.*

Neil seemed almost to have heard the grim prayer I'd managed not to utter.

"Keith couldn't have done anything to that little girl, Eric," he said emphatically. "He didn't have a car. Whoever took her, he had to have had a car. You don't just take a child from her house and walk away."

I saw the twin beams of a car once again sweep across the undergrowth. "I know."

A stream of images sped through my mind, Keith slouching down the walkway, brushing past the low-slung limbs of the Japanese maple at its far end, moving stealthily up the stairs. I recalled the way he'd frozen at the sound of my voice, then stood facing the door, his rumpled shirttail hanging halfway outside his pants. For an instant, the thought of why his shirt had been pulled from his trousers was almost more than I could bear.

Neil touched my arm softly. "Believe me, Eric, Keith's not a . . ." He stopped, considered his words, then said, "Keith wouldn't . . . hurt a little girl."

I nodded silently because there seemed nothing else to do, no words I could safely say. Then I went back to work. I framed Mrs. Phelps's photograph, then another and another as the hours passed and customers came and went, sometimes glancing in my direction, sometimes avoiding me altogether, both of which I found uncomfortable. It was a form of discomfort I didn't want Keith to experience, I decided, so at noon I called Meredith and told her that I thought it best that Keith go directly home after school until the matter of Amy Giordano was settled.

"I don't want him being looked at the way people are looking at me," I said. "Like an animal in the zoo."

"Of course," Meredith agreed. "Besides, with him the look would be even worse."

"What do you mean?"

Her answer chilled me with its unflinching starkness. "Like the cage door is unlocked," she said.

Warren arrived just as I was closing. He was dressed in coveralls, white cotton, dotted with paint. Bits of dried paint also clung to the wispy orange strands of his hair and dotted his hands and lower arms.

"Thought we might grab a beer, Bro," he said.

I shook my head tiredly. "It's been a long day, Warren. I think I'll just head home."

Neil swept by, said hello to Warren, then made his way toward the old green Dodge he'd more or less inherited from his mother.

Warren laughed. "Jesus, what a pansy," he said. He looked at me, the smile now gone. "I'd really like to have a beer, Eric." He didn't wait for me to refuse a second time. "The cops came by this house I was working on. Earl Bannister's place. They came right up to Earl and asked for me. Two cops. The ones that talked to you, I guess."

"Peak and Kraus."

"Sounds right," Warren said. "Anyway, that's not good, them coming up to Earl that way. I can't have cops coming around, asking for me while I'm on a job. Asking questions. Making it look like I'm . . . involved in something." His tone grew more tense and even a little resentful that he'd been drawn into circumstances he had not created but now knew no way to avoid. "I'm a housepainter, for Christ's sake. In and out of people's houses. You got to be trusted in this business, not be on the job and a couple of cops show up." His face reddened slightly. "It's got to stop, Eric," he said with sudden urgency. "I mean, I can't let this go on. We have to talk about it, you know?"

He was working himself up, getting more and more agitated. It was one of Warren's traits, a continual escalation until his emotions peaked and he either started sobbing, as he did when he was drunk, or fell asleep, as he did when he was sober.

"All right," I said. "Let's go over to Teddy's."

Teddy's was a small bar just a few doors down from my shop. Teddy Bethune, the owner, had died several years before, so that it was now run by his middle-aged daughter, a frowsy, irritable woman who had never made a secret of the fact that she actually preferred tourists to the boozy regulars who liked to sing old Irish songs, tell dirty jokes, and who continually regaled her with tales of how much more fun the bar had been before her father died.

"What'll you have?" Peg asked as she plopped two paper coasters before us.

We ordered two beers, grabbed the frosted bottles and headed for the booth at the back.

Warren took a long swig, then, before talking, decided on another. After that he put the bottle down on the table. "Hits the spot," he said.

"What did the cops want to know?" I asked.

"What I saw."

"You mean, Amy?"

"Amy, yeah, and Keith."

"Keith?"

"What he looked like." Warren took another swig from the bottle. "How he was acting. You know, like was he strange or anything that night. The short one was real interested in that."

"Peak," I said. "What did you tell him?"

"Like you told me, Eric. The truth."

"Which was?"

"That he was in a mood."

I stared at my brother, appalled. "Jesus, why did you say that?"

Warren looked at me, astonished. "Say what?"

"That Keith was in a mood. What the hell does that mean, anyway, that he was in a mood?"

Warren looked the way he did when he was twelve, and I was eight, his younger brother berating him for some stupid blunder.

"I figured I needed to tell them something," he said lamely. "You know, give them something. You always got to give them something, right?"

"Why do you think that?"

Warren didn't answer, but I knew he'd gotten the idea from television or the movies.

I slumped forward and ran my fingers through my hair. "All right, listen to me," I said wearily. "What exactly did you say?"

"Just what I told you," Warren answered.

He looked vaguely frightened, like a little boy who'd screwed up his part in the class play, and I remembered how cruelly my father had dismissed him, and how, to please my father, and to feel in league with him, I'd often adopted the same attitude toward my brother, exaggerating his failures, mocking his small successes. I couldn't help but wonder if in some way I was still locked in that adolescent pattern.

"Listen, Warren," I said, now trying for a less scolding tone. "A little girl is missing. This town is small, and this thing is getting bigger and bigger. You've seen her picture all over. There's even one on the door of my shop. And ribbons now.

Yellow ribbons all over town. That means the cops are under a lot of pressure. Their jobs are on the line. So they have to find Amy, dead or alive, and then they have to find whoever did this. See what I mean?"

Warren stared at me blankly.

"What I'm saying is that if they begin to think that Keith had something do with this, they'll hone in on him. They won't look anywhere else. They have to close the case."

Warren nodded slowly, his big soft eyes blinking languidly.

"Which means that Keith being 'in a mood' gives them something to think about, turn over in their minds, and so they start thinking, okay, we got this kid, a little weird, no friends . . . in a mood that night."

"So things start to add up to the cops," Warren said.

"Yes."

He took another sip from the beer, then nodded toward my bottle. "You not having any?" he asked, immediately shuffling off my warning, as well as any responsibility he might have for sinking my son deeper into police suspicion.

I pushed the bottle away. "What else did you tell them?" I asked sternly.

Warren stiffened, like a lowly private at an officer's approach. "Just that I drove Keith to the Giordanos' house," he said. "Amy was in the front yard. She came running up to the car. Then Keith got out and the two of them went inside." He hesitantly took another sip of beer. "Oh, and that I said hi to her."

"Anything else?"

"They wanted to know how she looked with Keith."

"Looked?"

"Like was she glad to see him, or did she act different when she saw him, like afraid, or backed away, stuff like that."

"What did you say?"

"I told them I didn't notice how she looked. Then they asked me if he touched her, you know, in a funny way, like maybe he shouldn't have, that kind of touch."

I dreaded the question but asked it anyway. "Did he?"

"No."

"Did he touch her at all?"

"He took her hand," Warren said. "He took her hand and led her inside."

"And that's it?"

"Yeah."

"Nothing else about Keith's mood?"

"No."

"You're sure you didn't say anything else, Warren."

"No, nothing," Warren assured me. Another swig. "What would I say?"

"I just need to know if there was anything else."

Warren shook his head with childish exaggeration. "Not a word, Eric." He lifted his hand. "I swear."

"Okay," I said, "Okay, that's not too bad then, I guess."

Warren took a swig and smiled like a little boy briefly in trouble but relieved now, all the burden lifted from him.

He chuckled. "But I got to admit, they made me nervous, those cops." He threw his head back, as if peering upward into the heart of some distant memory. "People like that always make me nervous."

I took a sip from my bottle, my own relief not all that different from Warren's, satisfied that he'd said nothing damaging about Keith.

"They all have the same look in their eyes, those guys," Warren added. "You know, suspicious."

I glanced at my watch, anxious to get home.

"Like that guy who came by the house after Mom's accident," Warren said. "The one we had, you know, when we lived in the big house."

He meant the house we'd lost, the one Dad had mortgaged to the hilt in his failed effort to regain financial ground, the one the bank had finally taken from us.

"I loved that house," Warren added. "Remember how we used to sail on the pond?"

"Yeah," I said.

"We'd already lost it when this guy came," Warren said. "I was packing boxes and he . . ."

"What guy are you talking about?"

"Some insurance guy."

"I don't remember any insurance guy coming to the house," I said.

"That's because you were with Aunt Emma."

I had been twelve years old the summer of my mother's death, and I recalled how my father had driven me across town to stay with his sister until, as he put it, "things calmed down."

"I stayed with Dad, remember?" Warren said. "Helping him pack."

My father had often enlisted Warren to do such heavy work, so it didn't surprise me that he'd used him as a kind of packhorse when he'd had to clean the house out before its repossession.

"Where was Dad when this guy came to the house?"

Warren shrugged. "You know Dad. He could have been anywhere." He looked at the empty bottle, then raised his hand and ordered another. "Anyway," he said. "With Dad not around, I didn't know what to do. But I figured, okay, this is just some guy from the insurance company, so, if he wants to talk to me, so what? I didn't see any harm in it."

"So you talked to him."

"Yeah. I was just a kid. He was a grown man. Big guy. You know, an adult. You don't say no, right?"

Peg arrived, plopped down Warren's beer then glared at me. "You?"

"I'm fine," I said.

She turned heavily and lumbered back up toward the front of the bar. "Besides, he was just asking about general stuff," Warren added. "Like how things were." He rolled the bottle between his hands, getting jumpy again, as if he suspected that I was laying some kind of trap for him. "You know, was Mom okay. Stuff like that. Family stuff. I didn't think much about it then, but it sort of gives me the creeps now."

"Why?'

"Because he seemed, you know, suspicious."

"Suspicious of what?"

"Us. I guess. Things in the family. Between Mom and Dad. Like, were things okay between them."

"He asked you that?"

"No, it was more a feeling I got, you know, like he was wondering if things were okay with them."

"What did you tell him?"

"That everything was fine," Warren said. "Which is why I couldn't understand why Dad got so pissed when I told him about this guy. Told me to keep my mouth shut, not let this guy in if he showed up again." He took a sip from the beer and wiped away a residue of white froth from his mouth with the back of his hand. "I guess he told the guy the same thing, because he never came back after that one time." He shrugged. "So whatever it was, it got settled, right?"

"Sounds like it," I answered. I glanced at my watch again. "I have to get home, Warren."

"Yeah, sure," Warren said. "I'll just hang around, finish my beer."

I got to my feet. "Just remember, if the cops talk to you again, be careful what you say."

Warren smiled. "You can count on me," he said.

TEN

Keith was in his room when I arrived at home.

"How'd he take it?" I asked Meredith. "My not wanting him to make deliveries for a while."

"I can't tell," Meredith answered. She was in the kitchen, standing at the cutting board, running a knife across the fleshy surface of a late-summer tomato. Its juices ran out onto the board and added a tang to the air. "He's just wears that same, flat face. No emotions. 'Flat affect'—that's what they call it."

"Who calls it that?"

"Psychologists."

"He's a teenager," I said. "All teenagers have 'flat affect.'"

She stopped slicing. "Did you?"

It was an unexpected question, but one I thought I could answer with a swift, decisive no. Then I recalled the moment when I'd been told of my mother's death, the way her car had plunged off a thirty-foot bridge. She'd been impaled on the steering wheel, a fact my father had not been reluctant to divulge, and yet, for all the gruesome nature of her death, I had simply nodded and walked upstairs to my room, turned on the phonograph, and listened to the album I'd just borrowed from a friend. Before now, I'd considered such behavior merely my way of choking off my grief, but now, thinking through it again, I couldn't be sure that I'd actually felt my mother's death as viscerally as I might have expected. At the funeral, for example, I'd sat silently beside my equally silent father, toying with my sleeve, while Warren sobbed uncontrollably, his fleshy shoulders shaking, huge tears running down his fat cheeks.

"Maybe I did," I admitted. "When my mother died, I didn't exactly fall apart."

"But I thought you loved your mother," Meredith said.

"I think I did," I said. "I mean, she was the one who wanted me to go to college, scrimped and saved."

I remembered how, even in the midst of our worsening financial situation, she'd hoarded a few pennies from each month's budget. She'd called it my college fund and had sworn me to secrecy, made me promise not to tell Warren and especially not to tell my father. It couldn't have been very much money, of course, and after her death I'd always assumed that my father had found it buried deep inside a closet or on the top shelf of the kitchen cabinet, then spent it in his usual way, probably on a final bottle of expensive brandy.

"I should have been really hurt by her death," I said. "But I don't remember being all that upset about it." I recalled the slow, deliberate tone my father had taken when he broke the news, his voice even, emotionless. He might as easily have been informing me of a sudden change in the weather. "My father didn't seem all that upset, either," I added.

Meredith looked as if I'd just revealed a formerly hidden aspect of my character. "Maybe that's where Keith gets it then." She began slicing the tomato again. "Anyway, it's not supposed to suggest anything, this flat affect behavior."

"What would it suggest?"

"You know, that he's a monster."

"Jesus, Meredith, Keith's not a monster."

She continued to slice the tomato. "That's what I just said."

I sat down at the kitchen table. "The cops talked to Warren. He told them Keith was in a mood that night."

Meredith spun around, the knife frozen in her hand. "What a fucking idiot," she snapped.

"Yeah."

"Goddamn it!"

"I know. I told him the next time to think before he spoke."

"As if he could," Meredith said hotly. "In a mood, Jesus Christ!" She seemed to smolder as she stood, knife in hand, glaring at me. "What's wrong with him, anyway? Is he just stupid, or is it something worse?"

"Something worse?"

"I mean, is he *trying* to get Keith in trouble?"

"Why would he do that?"

"Oh, come on, Eric." She put down the knife. "He's jealous of you. He always has been. You've always been the favorite. To your mother, but not just her. I mean, to this day, your father doesn't care if Warren comes by to see him. He never thinks about Warren. And then there's the fact that you have a wife, a son, a real family. What does Warren have? Absolutely nothing."

All of this was true, but I had never considered its corrosive effects before, the terrible possibility that all the years of feeling small and unsuccessful, of living in a tiny rented house alone, might have corrupted some aspect of my brother's heart, poisoned him against me so that he secretly reveled in my current troubles, perhaps even sought to deepen them.

"Do you really think Warren would deliberately try to implicate Keith in this thing with Amy?"

"Yes," Meredith answered bluntly.

The sheer force of her reply, the world of bitter envy it unearthed, was more than I could accept. "I just can't believe he'd do something like that, Meredith," I said.

Her gaze was withering, and beneath it I felt like a hopelessly clueless child. "You don't have any idea how malicious people really are, Eric," she said. "And I don't think you ever will."

There was no way to answer such a charge, and so I merely shook my head, walked into the living room, and turned on the television. The local news was just beginning. The lead story, once again, was about Amy's disappearance.

There'd been no developments in the case, the reporter said, but the police were busy following a few "promising leads."

Promising leads.

I glanced back to where Meredith stood at the entrance of the kitchen, her eyes fixed on the television screen.

"Promising leads," she repeated sarcastically. "I wonder how many of them came from dear old Warren."

I turned back to the television. By then, the report had gone live, with Peak and Kraus before a bristling array of microphones, Peak out front, Kraus standing stiffly behind him. For the next few seconds, Peak brought reporters up to date. The police, he said, were following a number of leads. A hotline had been established, and some of the information gained from callers appeared "credible."

"Credible," Meredith scoffed as she sat down on the sofa beside me. "Not if it came from Warren."

"Please, Meredith," I said quietly.

Peak ended his update by saying that the Giordanos were being fully cooperative, that they absolutely were not suspects in Amy disappearance, and that they'd recently turned over the family computer so police could see if Amy might have been contacted by "suspicious individuals" on the Internet.

With that, Peak turned, and started to go back into police headquarters.

"Do you have a suspect?"

The question had come from the crowd of reporters gathered on the steps of the building, but when he turned, Peak appeared to recognize the reporter who'd asked it.

"We're looking at several people," Peak said.

"But do you have one suspect in particular?" the reporter asked.

Peak glanced at Kraus, then faced the camera. "We're building a case," he said. "That's all I can tell you."

Then, almost like an apparition, he was gone.

"Building a case," Meredith said. She looked at me worriedly. "Against Keith."

"We don't know that," I told her.

She looked at me again in the way she'd looked at me when I'd denied my brother's ill intent. "Yes, we do," she said.

We had dinner an hour later, Keith slumped mutely in his chair, toying with his food, barely eating it. Watching him, I could not imagine Peak and Kraus building a case against him. In some sense, he appeared too pale and skinny to be considered a threat to anyone. But more than his physical weakness argued against his having done anything bad to Amy Giordano. Brooding silently at the table, aimlessly picking at his food, he gave off a sense of being innocuous, far too listless and desultory to have summoned the sheer malicious impetus required to harm a child. My son could not have hurt Amy Giordano, I decided, because he lacked the galvanizing energy necessary for such an act. He was too drab and ineffectual to be a child killer.

And so I forced myself to believe that the phantom suspect against whom the police were building their case had to be thick and burly, with a muscular body and short powerful legs. I wanted him to be a drifter or some visitor from another town. But barring that, I would have settled for anyone, as long as it wasn't Keith.

"How's school?" I asked, then regretted it since it was exactly the kind of inane parental question all teenagers dread.

"It's okay," he answered dully.

"Just okay?"

He plucked a single green bean from the rest of them as if he were playing a solitary game of pick-up-sticks. "It's okay," he repeated, his tone now somewhat sharp, like a felon impatient with interrogation.

"Is there anything we need to know about?" Meredith asked in her usual no-nonsense tone.

"Like what?" Keith asked.

"Like about Amy," Meredith answered. "Are you having any trouble over Amy?"

He drew another green bean from the stack, peered at it as if he thought it might suddenly begin to squirm, then let it drop back onto his plate. "Nobody says anything about it."

"At some point they might," Meredith said.

Keith picked lazily at a red pimple, but said nothing.

"Keith?" Meredith said insistently. "Did you hear me?"

His hand dropped abruptly into his lap. "Yeah, okay, Mom."

He remained silent for the rest of the meal, then excused himself with an exaggerated show of formality and returned to his room.

Meredith and I cleared the table, put the dishes in the dishwasher, and finally returned to the living room where we watched television for a time. Neither of us had much to say, nor did either appear uncomfortable in the silence. There was, after all, nothing to talk about but Keith, and that was a subject that could not be raised without heightening the general level of anxiety, and so we simply avoided it.

A few hours later we went to bed. Meredith read for a while. I knew she was trying to lose herself in a book. That had always been one of her ways of coping. During her mother's illness, she'd read continually, but never more than at her mother's hospital bedside, where she'd devoured book after book in a frantic effort to keep her mother's approaching death at bay. Now she was using the same tactic to keep from dwelling on the grim possibility that our son might be in very deep trouble.

Before she finally turned out the light, it was clear that this time the tactic had failed.

"Do you think Keith should see a counselor?" she asked. She turned toward me and propped her head up in an open palm. "There's one at the college. Stuart Rodenberry. Kids come to him with their troubles. People say he's very good."

"Keith wouldn't talk to a counselor," I said.

"How do you know?"

"He doesn't talk to anybody."

"But everyone wants to reach out, don't you think, to someone?"

"You sound like a counselor, yourself."

"I'm serious, Eric," Meredith said. "Maybe we should think about setting up something with Stuart."

I didn't know what to say, whether counseling was a good or bad idea at this point, and so I simply said nothing.

"Look," Meredith continued, "Stuart's going to be at Dr. Mays's party on Friday. I'll introduce you. If you think Keith might respond to him, we can go from there."

"Fair enough," I said.

With that, Meredith turned out the light.

I lay in the darkness, laboring to fall asleep. But sleep eluded me, and as time crawled forward, my mind drifted back to my first family, which, for all its tragedies, seemed less besieged by trouble. A sister dead at seven, a mother impaled upon a steering wheel, a destitute father living out his days in a modest retirement home, an alcoholic brother—these were, for all their misfortune, not problems unknown to other families. Other families had yet different problems, but those, too, now struck me as common, ordinary. In comparison, Keith's situation was much darker and more sinister. I couldn't shake the image of him slouching out of the shadows and into the house that night, then stealthily trudging up the stairs to face the door when I spoke to him, as if he were afraid to look me in the eye. There was something familiar in the scene, a sense that I'd lived through it before. But try as I did, I couldn't bring the earlier moment back until I suddenly remembered how, on the morning before Jenny's death, Warren had returned from Jenny's room where he'd been more or less stationed by my father to see her through the night. It wasn't a job he'd wanted, and he'd tried to get out of it, but my father had insisted. "You just have to sit by the goddamn bed, Warren," he'd barked, a clear suggestion that any more complex task would have been beyond my brother's limited capacity. Warren had gone to Jenny's room at midnight, then returned to his own room when my mother relieved him at six in the morning. He'd looked lost and bedraggled as he trudged down the corridor in the dawning light, his heavy footsteps awakening me so that I'd walked out into the hallway, where I saw him standing, facing the door, just as Keith had, his eyes fixed and unmoving, unable to look at me when I'd asked about Jenny, muttering only, "I'm going to bed," before he opened the door to his room and disappeared inside.

It was the similarity in those two scenes that struck me now, one that went beyond the stark choreography of two teenage boys tired and bedraggled, walking down a hallway, standing rigidly before the closed doors of their rooms. There was a similarity of mood, tone, a sense that these two boys were laboring under similar pressures, both of which had to do, I realized suddenly, with the fate of a little girl.

My anxiety spiked abruptly. I drew myself from the bed, walked out into the corridor, then down the stairs to the unlit kitchen, where I sat in the darkness and thought each scene through again and again, trying to locate some reason beyond the obvious one as to why they so insistently bore down upon me.

It came to me slowly, like the building light of dawn, darkness giving way to gray, then to steadily brightening light. The real similarity was not between the two scenes, but between my brother and my son, the fact, hard though it was for me to admit, that in some sense I thought of both of them as losers in life's cruel lottery, locked in failure and dis-appointment, members of that despised legion of middle-aged drunks and teenage geeks whose one true power, I thought, must be their unheralded capacity to control their own consuming rage.

He took her hand and led her inside.

Warren's words suddenly called another scene into my mind, Keith summoned by the Giordanos to babysit this daughter they so completely loved. Amy Giordano. Raven-haired, with flawless skin, smart, inquisitive, her future impossibly bright and radiant, destined to be one of life's winners.

Keith's words tore through my brain in a sudden, chilling snarl—*Princess Perfect.*

In my mind I saw Keith take Amy's hand and lead her inside the house. Could it be, I wondered, that her beauty and giftedness worked on him like an incitement, everything about her an affront, her shining qualities always in his face, goading him from the general sluggishness that would have otherwise stayed his hand.

My own stark whisper broke the air. *"Could he have hated her?"*

I felt another anxious spike, walked out into the yard, and peered up into the nightbound sky where, in the past, I'd sometimes found comfort in the sheer beauty of the stars. But now each glint of light only reminded me of the mysterious headlights of the car I'd seen that night. Now I imagined a mysterious figure behind the wheel, Keith on the passenger side, then I added a frightful third image, a little girl crouched naked on the floorboard, tied and gagged, whimpering softly if still alive, and, if not, stiff and silent, my son's unlaced tennis shoes pressed against her pale, unmoving face.

ELEVEN

It was a horrible vision, a fear for which I had no real evidence, and yet I couldn't rid myself of it. All through the night, I thought of nothing but that car, the ghostly driver, my son, all of it tied to the fact that Amy Giordano was incontestably missing and my growing suspicions that Keith had lied to me and to others for no reason I could figure out.

I alone knew about the car, of course, but by morning I also knew that it wasn't a knowledge I could keep to myself anymore. And so, just after Keith trooped down the stairs, mounted his bike, and headed off to school, I broke the news to Meredith.

"I think Keith may be hiding something," I blurted.

Meredith had already put on her jacket and was headed for the door. She froze and immediately faced me.

"He said he walked home that night, but I'm not sure he did."

"What makes you think he didn't?"

"I saw a car pull into the driveway up by the road," I said. "Then, just a few seconds later, Keith came walking down the drive."

"So you think someone brought him home that night?"

"I don't know," I answered. "Maybe."

"Did you see who the driver was?"

"No," I answered. "The car didn't pull all the way down the driveway."

"So you couldn't tell if Keith got out of that car?"

"No."

"Why didn't you tell me about this?"

"I don't know," I admitted. "Maybe I was afraid to—"

"Confront it?"

"Yes," I admitted.

She thought for a moment, then said, "We can't say anything about this, Eric. Not to the police or Leo. Not even to Keith."

"But what if he lied, Meredith?" I asked. "That's the worst thing he could have done. I told him that when I saw him in town the day the police were here. Before I brought him back. I told him that he had to tell the truth. If he didn't, then he has to . . ."

"No," Meredith repeated sternly, like a captain taking charge of a dangerously floundering vessel. "He can't take anything back. Or add anything. If he does, they'll keep at him. More and more questions. He'll have to lie again and again."

I heard it like distant thunder, dark and threatening, inexorably closing in. "Lie about what?"

She seemed to struggle for an appropriate answer, then gave up. "About that night."

"That night?" I asked. "You think he knows something about—?"

"Of course not, Eric," Meredith snapped. Her voice was strained and unconvincing, so that I wondered if, like me, she'd begun to entertain the worst possible suspicion.

"The problem, Eric," she added, "is that if they find out he lied, there'll be more questions. About him. About us."

"Us?"

"About why we covered it up."

"We're not covering anything up," I said.

"Yes, we are," Meredith said. "You've known about that car from the first night."

"Yes," I admitted, "But it's not as if I was trying to cover up something Keith did. Like hiding a bloody hammer, something like that. It was just a car. Keith might not even have been in it."

Meredith glared at me, exasperated. "Eric, you sat in our living room and listened to two cops question our son. You heard his answers, and you knew that one of them might have been a lie, but you didn't say anything." Her eyes flamed. "It's too late to take any of this back, Eric." She shook her head. "It's too late to take anything back."

For a moment I couldn't tell exactly what she was talking about, what, among perhaps scores of things, could not be taken back.

"All right," I said. "I won't say anything."

"Good," Meredith said. Then, with no further word, she whirled around, opened the door, and fled toward the car, the heels of her shoes popping like pistol shots on the hard brick walk.

Despite Meredith's conclusion that we couldn't say anything about the car I'd seen pull into our driveway that night, I thought of calling Leo Brock and telling him about it. But I never did. Meredith would no doubt argue that it was because I knew Leo would be irritated that I'd withheld something from him and I didn't want to confront that irritation.

But the reason is simpler even than that. The fact is, by midmorning I'd entered an irrational state of hope that it might all simply go away. This hope was based on nothing, and because of that I've come to believe that we are little more than machines designed to create hope in the face of doom. We hope for peace as the bombs explode around us. We hope the tumor will not grow and that our prayers will not dissolve into the empty space into which we lift them. We hope that love will not fade and that our children will turn out all right. As our car skids over the granite cliff, we hope, as we fall, that a cushion will receive us. And at the end, the last fibers of our hope throb for painless death and glorious resurrection.

But on that particular morning, my hope was more specific, and I have no doubt that it sprang from a groundless feeling that things were getting back to normal. Customers came and went, but none of them looked at me in precisely the same way as Mrs. Phelps had the day before. Instead, they nodded polite greetings, smiled, looked me dead in the eye. Perhaps the case was growing cold in their minds, the events distant, their former urgency dissipating. Perhaps my customers had come to accept the fact that Amy was missing and we might never know what had become of her. If this were so, then soon the flyers with Amy's picture would peel from the town's shop windows. The yellow ribbons would unravel and fall to the ground, to be picked up and tossed into the garbage. For a time, the people of Wesley would vaguely consider that my son might have had something to do with Amy's disappearance, but day by day, the stain of their suspicion would fade, and eventually his association with whatever had happened to Amy Giordano would fade as well, and we would all be back to where we were before that night. That was the illusion I allowed myself all that morning, so that by the time I came back from lunch, got out of my car, and headed toward the shop, I half believed that the worst was over.

Then suddenly, like a creature rising from dark, brackish water, he was there.

I saw him get out of the delivery van he used to haul his fruits and vegetables, the bright green cap and vest, his lumbering, muscular figure oddly hunched, like a man carrying a huge invisible stone.

"Hello, Vince," I said.

I could see what the last few days had done to him, the toll they'd taken. His eyes were red with lack of sleep, and large brown crescents hung beneath them. His face looked as if it were hung with weights, everything pulled down slightly.

"Karen didn't want me to talk to you," he said. "Cops probably wouldn't like it, either."

"Then maybe it's not a good idea," I said.

He steadied himself with a shifting motion, and had it been Warren, I would have suspected he'd been drinking. But as far as I knew, Vince Giordano was not a drinking man, especially one who'd have a bag on at one-thirty in the afternoon.

"Maybe it's not," he said. "I don't know, maybe it's not." He glanced toward my shop, then back at me. "But I got to."

He'd always had a ruddy complexion, but now I noticed that the side of his face looked as if it had been roughly scraped. I pictured him clawing at himself with an agonizing desperation, like an animal gnawing at its paw, frantic to escape the metal trap.

"Karen can't have more kids," he said. "Amy was hard. And after her, Karen can't have another one."

I nodded softly, but I could feel my skin tightening, becoming armor. "I'm sorry, Vince."

His eyes glistened. "I got to have Amy back," he said. "She was all we had, Eric. All we'll ever have. And we got to have her back . . . one way or the other." Again his eyes fled from me. He sucked in a long trembling breath, but continued to stare out across the parking lot. "If she's in some"—his voice broke—"some ditch or something, you know?" He looked at me pleadingly. "You know?"

"Yes," I said quietly.

"Some ditch where . . . animals can . . . where—" He suddenly staggered forward, leaned into me, buried his face in my shoulder, and began to sob. "Oh, Jesus," he cried. "I got to have her back."

I draped a single arm over his shoulder, and he drew away quickly, as if stung by an electric charge. "You tell him that, okay?" he said. "Keith." His eyes were dry now, a desert waste. "You tell him that I got to have her back."

"Keith doesn't know where Amy is, Vince," I said.

His gaze fixed on me like two hot beams. "Just tell him," he said.

I started to speak, but he spun around and made his way to his truck, his short powerful arms sawing the wind mechanically, like a furious wind-up doll.

"Keith doesn't know anything," I called after him.

Vince didn't turn, and when he reached his van, he yanked open the door and pulled himself in behind the wheel. For a moment, he sat, head dropped forward, eyes downcast. Then he turned toward me, and I saw the depth of his pain and knew beyond doubt that his world had shrunk to the dark, pulsing nucleus of Amy's loss. All that had mattered to him before no longer mattered. Nor did all that still mattered to others touch him now. I heard his words again, fraught with desperate warning, *I got to have her back*. Beneath the anguish, there was a festering rage. Vince would level cities, vaporize oceans, burn all the fields of earth to hold Amy in his arms again, hold her dead or alive. For him, all existence weighed no more than sixty pounds, stood no higher than four feet. Everything else was dust.

I didn't want to go into the shop after that, didn't want Neil to see how shaken I was. He'd ask questions I didn't want to answer. And so I walked to the other end of the mall and dialed Leo Brock.

"I had a little . . . confrontation with Vince Giordano," I told him.

"When?"

"Just now."

"Where?"

"In the parking lot outside my shop."

"What did he say?"

"That he wants Amy back," I answered. "He told me to tell that to Keith."

"I see."

"He thinks Keith did something, Leo," I added. "He's convinced himself of that."

There was a pause, and I could almost hear the tumblers of Leo's brain.

"Listen, Eric," he said at last. "The police seem to think that there's something wrong. Something somebody isn't telling."

"What do you mean?"

"That's the most I could get out of my source," Brock said. "Nothing concrete. Just a feeling that something's wrong."

"With Keith?"

"With something," Leo said. "The guy who tells me these things, he just gives hints."

"Something wrong," I repeated. "Where would they come up with an idea like that?"

"I don't know. Maybe they got a tip."

"A tip? From whom?"

"It could be anybody," Leo answered. "It could have come from that hotline they've set up. You know how that works. Anonymous. Anybody can call in, say anything."

"But the cops don't have to believe it, do they?"

"No, they don't," Leo said. "But if it has any credibility, then they're apt to look into it. Especially in a case like this. Missing girl. They're under a lot of pressure, Eric, as I'm sure you know." He paused, like a priest in the confessional, using silence as a spade, digging at me. "So, if you know of something . . . wrong."

I choked back the reflex to tell him about the car. "This isn't enough," I said. "This isn't enough for me to go on, this business of something being wrong. Jesus Christ. It could be anything. Something 'wrong.' Jesus, could they get more vague?"

"Which is why I'm asking," Leo said.

"What exactly are you asking, Leo?"

"Eric, listen," Leo said evenly. "This business of Vince Giordano, don't worry about that. I can get a restraining order in two seconds. But understand, on this other matter, the police are going to be looking into things."

"What things?"

"Whatever looks promising from their point of view," Leo said. "They don't have to go in only one direction. If something comes in, like on that hotline, they can run with it. It could be anything. Some rumor. This is a police investigation, Eric, not a trial. The rules aren't the same."

I shook my head. "Hotline. Jesus Christ. Just something somebody says over the phone, and—"

"That's right," Leo interrupted. "So let me ask you this, is there any reason why someone out there might want to hurt you or Meredith?"

"By doing what? Blaming this whole thing on Keith?"

"Perhaps that. Or maybe just by planting stories."

"What kind of stories?"

"Any story that might get the attention of the police."

I laughed coldly. "Like we're drug dealers . . . or Satanists?"

Leo's tone was grave. "Anything, Eric."

Suddenly I felt drained, all my energy dissipated, my earlier optimism flattened like an animal on the road. "God," I breathed. "My God."

"I don't know what this 'something wrong' is," Leo said. "My guess, it's probably nothing. But they don't need much, the cops. Not in a case like this."

I lifted my head slightly, like a battered fighter rallying before the next bell. "Well, the answer is no," I said. "There is nothing wrong."

After a pause, Leo said, "All right." He cleared his throat roughly. "Do you want me to take action regarding Mr. Giordano?"

I saw Vince's stricken face bury itself in my shoulder, felt the tremble of his sobs. "No," I said. "Not yet."

"All right," Leo said again, his tone the same as seconds before, carrying a hint of disappointment. "But let me know if he approaches you again."

"I will," I assured him.

He hung up with no further word, but a mood continued to reverberate around me, weird suggestions about "someone out there" who might want to hurt me or Meredith or Keith, strike at our little family circle, rip it apart. I heard a whispered voice, anonymous and malicious, recorded on the police hotline, mouthing accusations of incest, abuse, all manner of deviance, but the longer the list became, the more I dismissed the dark accusing voice. Charges had to be proved, after all. Suspicion alone could not destroy anything.

Or could it?

Suddenly another question sliced through my brain, one directed not toward Keith or Meredith, as should have been expected, but to the mysterious man who'd shown up at the house, asked Warren questions, come on an insurance matter only a week or so after my mother's car had shattered the guardrail of the Van Cortland Bridge and plunged into the icy stream below.

What, I wondered with an inexplicable sense of dread, had he been looking for?

TWELVE

For the first time in years, I didn't want to go home that night, though even then, despite my anxiety, I had no idea that before long I would be leaving my home for good.

I saw it for the last time on a chill October day. The closing was set for that afternoon, and the new owner, an attorney with a young wife and two small children, was anxious to move in. I walked through the swept and empty rooms one by one, first the kitchen and living room, then upstairs to the bedroom Meredith and I had shared for so long. I looked out its frosted window to a carpet of fallen leaves. Then I walked out into the corridor where I'd faced Keith that night, passed through the door he'd slunk behind, and stared out the window over which he'd once hung a thick impenetrable shade, the one I'd finally ripped down in a fit of rage, my words at that moment once again echoing in my mind, *No more fucking lies!*

Perhaps I'd actually begun to sense that steadily approaching violence the evening I decided not to go home directly after work, but called Meredith instead, told her I was going to be late and tried to lose myself in the repetitive labor of safely enclosing idyllic family photographs within neat square walls of perfectly stained wood and painted metal. Or perhaps I'd begun to feel that the protective walls that had once surrounded my own family, both the first and the second, were beginning to crumble, and that if I could simply ignore the leaks and fissures, then it would all go away and Amy would be returned to Vince and Karen and I could return to Meredith and Keith and by that means escape the ghosts of that other family, Dad and my mother, Jenny and Warren, who'd already begun to speak to me in the same suspicious whisper I imagined as the voice on the police hotline, sinister, malicious, ceaselessly insisting that something at the heart of things was wrong.

I don't remember how long I remained in the shop after closing, only that night had fallen by the time I locked up and walked to my car. Neil had lingered briefly, needlessly shelving stock, so that I knew he was keeping an eye on me, ever ready to provide what he called a friendly shoulder. He left just after seven. I worked another hour, perhaps two, time somehow flowing past me without weight or importance, so that I felt as if I were adrift on its invisible current, a frail rudderless craft moving toward the distant haze behind which waits the furiously cascading falls.

I sat down behind the wheel, but didn't start the engine. All the stores in the mall were closed, and briefly I peered from one unlit shop window to the next. What was I looking for? Direction, I suppose. I knew that strange suspicions were now rising like a noxious mist around my first family, but I also knew that I had to let them go, concentrate on the far more serious matter that now confronted my second family. So, what was I looking for? Probably a way of thinking through the current crisis, putting it in perspective, running the various scenarios, everything from Amy found to Amy murdered, from Keith exonerated to the look on his face as they led him into the death chamber. No thought was too optimistic nor too grim for me that night as I careened from hope to gloom. The fact is, I knew nothing concrete, save that I'd seen a car at the end of the driveway then Keith moving through the darkness toward home.

Suddenly, Leo Brock's voice sounded in my mind: *Were you ever over around the water tower?*

Keith's answer had been typically short—*no*.

And yet, between the question and the answer, something had glimmered in my son's eyes, the same dark flaring I'd seen when he'd said that he'd walked home alone the night of Amy's disappearance.

I'd let all of this go for days, despite the fact that Amy's pajamas had been discovered in the general area of the tower, a fact I'd hardly thought about until that evening, when I suddenly felt the urge to go there, see the place for myself, perhaps even find some small thing, a lock of hair, a scrap of paper, that would lead me to her. It was an absurd hope, as I knew even then, but I'd reached the point where absurdity joined with reality, my son accused, however vaguely, of a terrible crime, and I unable to feel certain that he was not also guilty of it. That was the pressure that drove me forward, made me start the engine, drive out of the parking lot in front of my shop, turn right, and head toward the northern edge of town where, within minutes, I could see the top of the water tower glowing softly in the distance, motionless, cylindrical, like a hovering spacecraft.

The unpaved road that led to the tower was a bumpy winding one that grew ever more narrow as I drove down it. Two walls of green vines crept in from both sides of the road, sometimes clawing at my window like skeletal fingers.

The road curled to the left, then made a long circle around the looming tower and the high metal legs that supported its enormous weight. There were no formal parking spaces, but I could see indentations in the surrounding vegetation, places where cars had pulled in and parked with sufficient regularity to leave their ghostly images in the undergrowth.

I followed the road on around, then stopped, backed into a phantom space, and cut my lights. Now there was nothing to illuminate the darkness but the beams that swept down from the outer rim of the tower.

For a time I sat in that covering darkness, my gaze moving about the softly illuminated area beneath the tower. It was weedy and overgrown, and the wind rippled softly through the grasses. Here and there bits of litter tumbled briefly in these same breezes, then gently came to rest.

I saw nothing that I might not have expected of such a place. It was lonely and deserted and far off the beaten track, but beyond these common characteristics, it might have been reproduced in a dozen other towns throughout the region. They all had their own water towers, and nothing distinguished this one from those others except my gathering sense that it was used in some way, a designated meeting place, the sacred territory of a secret society. I half expected to see animal bones scattered about the grounds, the remains of some occult group's bizarre religious sacrifices.

That thought gave me an eerie chill, the feeling that I'd stumbled into someone else's territory, the way casual hikers are said to stumble onto marijuana patches in the middle of otherwise perfectly innocuous fields and meadows. Could it be, I wondered, that Amy Giordano had been brought here not merely because it was secluded, but for some specific purpose? My imagination fired luridly, and I saw her standing, stripped and bound, surrounded by a circle of robed figures, all of them mumbling satanic incantations as they slowly circled her. Then, in my mind's bizarre scenario, she was laid upon a makeshift altar, silver blades raised high above her as the incantation reached a fever pitch. Then the knives came down one at a time, each figure taking his appointed turn until—

That was when I saw the light.

It came down the same unpaved road I'd taken only minutes before, headlights bouncing jerkily as the car bumped toward the tower. At the tower, it circled slowly, the shadowy driver staring straight ahead as the car drifted past mine, so that I caught the face only in brief black silhouette.

Clearly, he was familiar with the place, because he drove directly to what seemed a preordained spot, then stopped, backed up, and turned off his lights.

I had backed deeply into the undergrowth, and so I doubt that he saw me as he passed, though surely he must have glimpsed the front of my car when he backed into his own place. If so, my presence did not in the least alarm him. Through the eerie haze cast beneath the tower, I saw him as he sat in the shadowy interior of his car. He did not get out, and for a time he remained almost completely still. Then I saw a slight movement and after that, the fire of a match and the glowing tip of a cigarette, rhythmically brightening and dimming with each inhalation.

The minutes passed, and as they did, the man became less sinister. I imagined him a harmless night owl, maybe plagued by an unhappy home, and so he'd found a place where he could sit alone, undisturbed, and either think things through or let his troubles briefly slip his mind altogether.

Then, out of the darkness, a second car made its approach, moving slowly, its headlights joggling through the undergrowth until it made the same slow turn, found its place, and backed in.

A woman got out, short and somewhat overweight, her blond hair hanging stiffly, like a wig. She walked to the second car and pulled herself in on the passenger side. Despite the darkness, I could see her talking with the man. Then she leaned forward, curling downward, and disappeared from view. The man took a final draw on his cigarette and tossed it out the window. The woman surfaced briefly, and I think they both laughed. Then she curled forward and disappeared again, this time without resurfacing until the man suddenly thrust his head backward and released what even from a distance I recognized as a shuddering sigh.

I wanted to leave, of course, to skulk away unseen, because there is a kind of intrusion that comes very close to crime. I felt like a thief, someone who'd broken into a secret chamber, and for that reason I remained in place, my head down, my eyes roaming here and there, avoiding the two cars that rested in the darkness several yards away. The sound of a car door returned me to them. The woman had gotten out of the man's car and was heading back toward her own. On the way, she grabbed the purse that dangled from her shoulder, opened it, and put something inside. Seconds later, she pulled away, the other car falling in behind her, both cars making their way around the circle, through the grasping vines, and back out onto the main road.

Even then, I stayed in place for fear that if I left too soon I might come upon one or the other of them and reveal what I'd seen at the tower.

Five minutes went by, then ten, and at last it seemed safe to leave. I drove back to the main road and headed home to where I knew I would find Meredith reading in bed and Keith secreted in his room, listening to music or playing his computer games. I thought I knew the things that were on Meredith's mind, either Keith or some problem at the college. But

Keith was much more of an enigma now, a boy who smoked, cursed, perhaps even lied to the police and me about—I couldn't even say how many things he might have lied about. I only knew that I couldn't stop my own growing suspicion that the anonymous caller on the police hotline had been right, that there was something wrong.

THIRTEEN

The next morning Keith left for school at his usual time. From the front window I watched as he mounted his bicycle and peddled up the short incline to the main road. Physically, he was burdened by nothing more than the book bag that hung at his back, but I couldn't help but consider the other weights he bore—confusion, isolation, loneliness. Still, these were no more than the usual burdens of a teenage boy, and I worked to dismiss any doubts that they might not be the only ones he carried.

"Well, I guess no news is good news."

I turned to see Meredith standing a few feet behind me, her gaze following Keith as he made his way up the incline and disappeared behind a wall of forest undergrowth.

"Nothing new from the cops," she added. "I guess that's a good thing."

I continued to peer out into the woods. "I suppose," I said dryly.

She cocked her head to the right. "You sound pessimistic, Eric. That's not like you." She came over and drew me around to face her. "You okay?"

I smiled weakly. "I'm just tired, that's all. Thinking about everything."

"Sure," Meredith said. "And it couldn't have been a very good experience, Vince Giordano coming up to you like that." She placed her hands on either side of my face. "Listen, we'll go to Dr. Mays's party tomorrow night, get out of this gloom, have a good time. We both need it, right, a chance to relax?"

"Yes."

With that she kissed me, though dartingly, spun around, and headed up to our bedroom to finish dressing.

I remained at the window, watching the morning light slant through the overhanging trees. I had never actually noticed how beautiful it was, the small piece of woodland that surrounded our house. For a moment I recalled the day we'd moved in, how before unloading the truck we'd taken a moment to stand and look around, Meredith with Keith beside her, how bright the day had been. How on that day, as we'd huddled together in this perfect wood, we had all been smiling.

It was a Thursday morning, and so, rather than drive directly to the shop, I headed for the retirement home where my father had lived for the past four years. I'd dropped in on him at exactly the same day and time since he'd first taken up residence there. Even in old age, he'd maintained his aversion to what he called "untimely surprises," by which he meant everything from a gift offered on any but appropriate occasions to unscheduled visits by either of his two sons.

That morning he received me as he always did, in a wheelchair parked on the home's broad front porch. Even in winter, he preferred that we sit outside, though in recent years, he'd given in a little on that one, and so from time to time I'd found him in the front room, his chair placed a few feet from the fireplace.

"Hello, Dad," I said as I came up the stairs.

"Eric," he said with a crisp nod.

I sat down in the wicker rocker beside his chair and glanced out over the grounds. They were roughly tended, dotted with crabgrass and dandelions, and I could see how much they offended him.

"They'll wait for frost to kill the weeds," he grumbled.

He'd always been a stickler that the spacious grounds surrounding the grand house on Elm Street were always perfectly manicured. He'd hired and fired at least ten groundskeepers during as many years. They were lazy or inept, according to him, though he'd never permitted my mother to so much as pick up a spade to correct their deficiencies. Her job had been to maintain my father, see to it that his suits were pressed, his desk cleared, his dinner on the table when he triumphantly returned home each evening. A woman's work, he'd pointedly declared, is always to be done on the inside.

"I guess you heard about Amy Giordano," I said.

He continued to stare out across the unkempt grounds.

"The little girl who disappeared," I added.

He nodded, but with little interest

"I guess you've also heard that Keith was babysitting her that night," I said.

My father's lips jerked downward, "He was bound to get in trouble," he said sourly. "This or something else."

I'd never guessed that my father had any such opinion of my son.

"Why do you think that?" I asked.

My father's eyes drifted over to me. "You never stood up to him, Eric," he said. "You never made him mind you. Same with Meredith. Hippies."

"Hippies?" I laughed. "Are you kidding me? I was never a hippie. I went to work when I was sixteen, remember? I didn't have time to be a hippie."

He turned back toward the yard, his eyes now strangely hard. "From the first time I saw him, I knew he'd be trouble."

In all the fifteen years of my son's life, my father had never expressed such a grim notion. "What are you talking about?" I demanded. "Keith has always been a good kid. Not the best grades, but a good kid."

"Looks like a bum," my father growled. "Like he lives on the street. Lazy. Like Warren."

"Warren's been good to you, Dad."

"Warren is a bum," my father sneered.

"When he was a kid, he worked his ass off for you."

"A bum," my father repeated.

"He did all the heavy lifting around the house," I insisted. "Every time you fired yet another landscaper, he took up the slack—mowed, cut the hedge. You even had him paint the house one summer."

"Looked like a melted cake when he finished," my father snarled. "Dripping all over. Splotches. Couldn't do corners. Messed up the latticework. Everything sloppy."

"Okay, so he didn't do a professional job," I said. "But he was just a kid, Dad. Sixteen years old that last summer."

That last summer. I remembered it with almost disturbing clarity. My father had been gone for days at a time, off to New York or Boston in search of cash. My mother had kept the house running by sheer will, secretly borrowing money from Aunt Emma, according to Warren, cutting corners at the grocery store, driving thirty miles to buy clothes at the Catholic thrift shop in a neighboring town.

"You refused to admit how bad things were," I reminded him. "You came back from New York with two new suits from Brooks Brothers."

My father waved his hand dismissively. "Nobody went hungry."

"We might have," I said. "If it hadn't been for Mom handling the household budget."

My father laughed coldly. "Your mother couldn't handle anything"—he waved his hand—"worthless."

"Worthless?" I asked, angry that he would say such a thing about a woman who'd spent her life taking care of him. "If she was so worthless, why did you have her insured?"

My father's head jerked to attention. "Insured?"

"Warren said there was insurance. When Mom got killed."

"What would Warren know about that?"

"The insurance man came to the house," I said.

I saw my father's face tighten slightly.

"He came one day when Warren was packing everything after the bank took the house."

My father laughed dryly. "Warren's nuts. There was no insurance man."

"According to Warren he was asking about our family, how things were between you and Mom."

"Bullshit!" my father grumbled, his voice now a low growl, like a dog driven into a corner.

I started to speak, but his hand shot up, stopping me. "What does a drunk like Warren know? His brain is soaked in alcohol." He lowered his hand, leaned back in his chair, and glared out over the weedy yard. "Nothing," he said bitterly. "When that old woman died, I got nothing."

"That old woman?" I repeated. "Jesus, Dad, she was devoted to—"

"Devoted to me?" my father bawled. His head rotated toward me with an eerie smoothness, and a caustic laugh burst from him. "You have no idea," he said.

"About what?"

My father chuckled to himself. "You don't know a thing about her. Devoted, my ass."

"What are you getting at?"

His laughter took a still more brutal turn, becoming a hard, hellish cackle. "Christ, Eric." He shook his head. "You always put her on a pedestal, but, believe me, she was no fucking saint."

"A saint is exactly what she was," I insisted.

His eyes twinkled with some demonic inner light. "Eric, trust me," he said. "You have no idea."

I was numb when I left him a few minutes later, numb and floating like a feather in the air. After his outburst, my father had refused to say anything more about my mother. It was as if their married life was a brief, unpleasant episode for him, a game of poker he'd lost or a horse he'd bet on that came in last. I remembered the effusive show of love and devotion he'd always put on for the well-heeled business associates who occasionally dropped by for a game of billiards or to sip his expensive scotch while they talked and smoked cigars in the grand house's well-appointed parlor. "And this is my beautiful bride," he'd say of my mother by way of introduction. Then, in an exaggerated gesture of adoration, he'd draw her to his side, cup her narrow waist in his hand . . . and smile.

It was just after ten when I arrived at the shop. Neil was already at work, as usual. A less-observant man might not have noticed any change in my demeanor, but Neil had always been quick to gauge even the subtlest alteration of mood. He saw the distress I was laboring to hide, but when he finally addressed the matter, he was miles off the mark.

"Business will pick up," he said. "People are just . . . I don't know . . . they're strange."

Strange.

The word abruptly swept away all my defenses, all my efforts to keep my fears in check. The dam broke, and I felt myself hurling forward on a rush of boiling dread, every dark aspect of the last few days now rising before me, demanding to be heard.

"Something wrong, boss?" Neil asked.

I looked into his hugely caring eyes and felt that I had no one else to go to. But even then, I had no idea where to begin. There was too much boiling within me now, too much hissing steam. I could barely sort one troubling doubt from another. And so I drew in a quick breath, trying to center myself and concentrate on the most immediate matter before me. Which surely, I decided, was Keith.

"I'd like to ask you something, Neil," I began tentatively.

"Anything," Neil said softly.

I walked to the front of the shop, turned out the CLOSED sign and locked the door.

Neil suddenly looked frightened. "You're going to fire me." His voice edged into panic. "Please don't, Eric. I'll correct whatever it is. I need this job. My mother, you know. Medicine. I—"

"It's not about the job," I assured him. "You do a great job."

He looked as if he were about to faint. "I know it wasn't a great summer, businesswise, but . . ."

"It has nothing to do with the shop," I said. I stopped and drew in a fortifying breath. "It's about Keith."

Neil's face grew very still.

I could find no alternative to simply leaping in. "What do you know about him?"

"Know about him?" Neil asked, clearly a little baffled by the curious urgency he heard in my voice.

"About his life."

"Not very much, I guess," Neil answered. "He talks about music, sometimes. What bands he likes, that sort of thing."

"Has he ever talked about girls?" I asked.

"No."

"How about friends? He doesn't seem to have any friends."

Neil shrugged. "He's never mentioned anyone."

"Okay," I said. "How about the people he delivers to. Have you ever heard any complaints?"

"What kind of complaints?"

"Anything about him, anything he did that seemed . . . strange."

Neil shook his head violently. "Absolutely not, Eric. Never!"

I looked at him pointedly. "You're sure?"

"Yes, I'm sure."

I nodded. "Okay," I said. "I just thought he might have come to you. I mean if—"

"If what?"

"If he had any . . . problems he wouldn't know how to deal with."

"What kind of problems?" Neil asked. He looked genuinely baffled. "I mean, he wouldn't talk to me about girls, right?"

"I guess not."

He looked at me curiously. "It bothers you, doesn't it? That Keith doesn't have a girlfriend?"

I nodded. "Maybe a little. Meredith says it does, but I'm not so sure. I mean, what if he doesn't have a girlfriend. He's just a kid. That doesn't mean he's—"

"Gay?"

"No," I said. "Not just that."

Neil heard the awkwardness in my voice, the sense of trying to weasel out of the truth. "Do you think Keith's gay?"

"I've thought about it," I admitted.

"Why? Has he said anything?"

"No," I answered. "But he seems angry all the time."

"What does that have to do with being gay?" Neil asked.

"Nothing."

No one had ever looked at me the way Neil did now, with a mixture of pain and disappointment. "Yeah, okay," he said softly.

"What?"

He didn't answer.

"What, Neil?"

Neil laughed dryly. "It just seems like you thought maybe if Keith was gay, he'd have to be angry. Hate himself, you know, that sort of thing. A lot of people have that idea. That a gay guy would have to hate himself."

I started to speak, but Neil lifted his hand and silenced me.

"It's okay," he said. "I know you don't believe that."

"No, I don't," I told him. "Really, Neil, I don't."

"It's okay, Eric," Neil repeated. "Really. It is." He smiled gently. "Anyway, I hope everything works out all right for everyone," he said quietly. "Especially for Keith."

He turned back toward the front of the shop.

"Neil," I said. "I didn't mean to . . ."

He didn't bother to look back. "I'm fine" was all he said.

———

For the rest of the day, customers came and went. Neil kept himself busy and seemed determined to keep his distance from me.

At five the color of the air began to change, and by six, when I prepared to lock up, it had taken on a golden glow.

The phone rang.

"Eric's Frame and Photo."

"Eric, they're coming here again," Meredith told me.

"Who?"

"The police. They're coming to the house again."

"Don't panic," I said. "They were there before, remember?"

I heard the fearful catch in her breath. "This time they have a search warrant," she said. "Come home."

PART III

Y ou stop now. You take a sip of coffee. You are halfway through the story you intend to tell. You realize that you have reached the moment when the lines you thought ran parallel begin to intersect. You know that from here on the telling will become more difficult. You will need to speak in measured tones, make the right connections. Nothing should blur, and nothing should be avoided. Particularly the responsibilities, the consequences.

You want to describe how the history of one family stained another, as if the colors from one photograph bled onto another in an accidental double exposure. You want to expose this process, but instead you stare out at the rain, watching people as they stand beneath their soaked umbrellas, and consider not what happened, but how it might have been avoided, what you could have done to stop it, or at least to change it in a way that would have allowed lives to go on, find balance, reach the high wisdom that only the fallen know.

But the wheels of your mind begin to spin. You can feel them spinning, but there is nothing to do but wait until they find traction. Then, without warning, they do, and you understand that all you can do is go on, start at exactly where you left off.

FOURTEEN

Come home.

I often repeat the words in my mind. I recall Meredith's caught breath each time I repeat them, hear the icy dread in her voice.

I hear other things, too—a whispery voice, a gunshot—and with those sounds I recognize that I've gone through all of it again, reliving every detail from that first night when Keith and Warren strolled down the walkway and disappeared behind the Japanese maple to the moment when I passed under that same tree for the last time. In retrospect, I suppose, everything seems inevitable, the whole course of events summed up in the grim irony of that line of poetry I read while I waited for Keith to come home from Amy Giordano's house that night— *"After the first death, there is no other."*

But there was.

I drove home quickly after Meredith's call. The sun was just setting when I pulled into the driveway, the air beneath the spreading limbs of the Japanese maple already a delicate pink. Meredith met me halfway up the walkway.

"I sent Keith into town. Because I needed to concentrate on writing a lecture. That's what I told him. He knows not to come back for a few hours." There were tiny creases at the sides of her eyes, as if she'd aged several years during the brief time between her phone call and my arrival. "I didn't tell him the police were coming over. I was afraid he might do something. Hide something."

I looked at her quizzically.

"It could be anything," she added. "Some dirty magazine, pot, anything he wouldn't want them to see. And if he did that, you know, not even thinking about it, it would still be obstruction of justice."

"I see you've talked to Leo."

"Yes," Meredith said. "I told him I was going to send Keith to the store, keep him out of his room. He thought it was a good idea."

"Because he doesn't trust Keith," I said. "That's why he thought it was a good idea."

Meredith nodded. "Probably."

"Is he coming over?"

"Only if the cops want to question Keith." She looked at me worriedly. "I don't want to talk to them, either. Especially Kraus. On the phone, he sounded hard—like we're the enemy?" She looked at me pleadingly. "Why would he act like that, Eric?"

"Maybe he doesn't think we're exactly ordinary," I said cautiously. "Did Leo mention the hotline? Things people might have said?"

"Said about what?"

"About us," I told her. "He has a source somewhere. With the police, I guess. And this source, whoever it is, told him that the police had gotten the idea that there was something wrong. Those were his words—*something wrong.* He thought somebody might have called on the hotline, told the cops something about us."

Meredith looked stricken, helpless, a small creature caught in a vast web.

"Leo has no idea what might have been said," I added. "But with the police under all this pressure, he's worried they'll believe just about anything they hear about us."

Meredith remained locked in grim silence, but I could see her mind working.

"Maybe someone saw that car pull into our driveway."

"Maybe," Meredith muttered.

"And there's something else they might have seen," I told her. "Remember when Leo asked Keith if he'd ever been around the water tower? I'm not sure Keith told the truth when he said no."

"What makes you think he didn't tell the truth?"

"Just the look in his eyes," I said. "It was the same one he had when he told the cops he came home alone." I shrugged.

"Anyway, the water tower, it's sort of a meeting place . . . for men and . . . prostitutes—or at least I think they're prostitutes. She was putting something in her bag. My guess is it was money."

Meredith looked dazed.

"I went there," I said. "To the water tower. Leo brought it up, and then the way Keith looked when he said he'd never been there, I just got curious."

"And you saw all this?" Meredith asked. "These men and—"

"Yes," I answered. "I don't know why Keith goes there. I mean, if he does. Maybe he just watches. Maybe that's his . . . outlet."

For a moment. Meredith seemed unable to deal with the tawdriness of what I'd just told her. "Okay, so there's this place and people go there. But why are you so quick to believe that Keith goes there . . . to watch . . . or for any other reason?"

I had no answer, and she saw that I had no answer. "Oh, Eric," she said exhaustedly. "What's happening to us?"

Meredith had put on her tightly controlled, professorial face by the time Peak and Kraus arrived. They brushed past the limbs of the maple and strode down the walkway at a leisurely pace, chatting to each other like two men on their way to the local tavern.

I met them at the door, and the instant I opened it, I noticed that their easy manner changed to one of cool professionalism. Now they stood erect, with somber faces, hands folded in front of them.

"Sorry to trouble you again, Mr. Moore," Peak said.

Kraus nodded to me, but said nothing.

"How do we do this?" I asked. "I've never had my house searched."

"We have a warrant for the house and grounds," Peak explained. "We'll try not to disturb anything unnecessarily."

"So I just let you in, is that it?"

"Yes."

I stepped back, swung the door open, and let them pass into the living room where Meredith stood, her body completely rigid, eyes not so much hostile as wary.

"Keith isn't home," she said. "We haven't told him about this."

"We won't be long," Peak said with a weak smile.

"Where do you want to start?" I asked.

"Keith's room," Peak said.

I nodded toward the stairs. "Second door on your left."

Meredith and I walked into the kitchen while Peak and Kraus searched Keith's room. Meredith made a pot of coffee, and we sat at the table and drank it silently. For that brief interval, we merely waited, held in suspension, staring at each other briefly, then drawing our gazes away. We might have been figures in a pantomime of a couple who'd been together too long, knew each other too well, and so had fallen into a final muteness.

Over the next few minutes, other officers arrived, all of them in uniform.

From our place in the kitchen, we watched as they poked about the yard, as well as the conservation forest that stretched for several acres behind our house. Two hours passed before Peak and Kraus came back down the stairs. Two young uniformed officers trailed behind them, carrying sealed bags stenciled in black letters: EVIDENCE.

I had no idea what the bags contained until Peak handed me a slip of paper on the way out. "That's the inventory of what we took from Keith's room," he said. "And of course we'll bring back anything that has no evidentiary value."

Evidentiary value, I thought. Evidence against Keith.

I glanced up the stairs and saw a uniformed officer coming down, carrying my son's computer.

"The computer in Keith's room," Peak said. "Is that the only one in the house?"

"No," I said.

"I'm afraid we'll have to look at them all," Peak said.

"There's one down the hall, in my office," Meredith said. "And I have a computer at college. Do you want to seize that, too?"

"Nothing is being seized, Mrs. Moore," Peak answered mildly. "But to answer your question, no, we have no need to take your computer." He paused, then added significantly, "At least, for now."

The police left a few minutes later, just as Keith was coming down the drive on his bike. He pulled over to the side, got off the bike, and watched the cars go by.

"What did the cops want this time?" he asked as he came into the house.

"They searched your room," I told him. "They took a few things." I handed him the inventory.

He scanned the list with surprising lack of interest until suddenly his eyes widened. "My computer?" he cried. "They have no right—"

"Yes, they do," I interrupted. "They can take anything they want."

He looked at the inventory again, but now with a sense of helplessness. "My computer," he muttered. He slapped the paper against the side of his leg. "Shit."

Meredith had been standing silently a few feet away, observing Keith no less intently than I was. Now, she stepped forward. "Keith, it's going to be okay." Her tone of sympathy surprised me, as if she somehow understood his fear, knew what it was like to be threatened with exposure. "It really is."

Now it seemed up to me to state the hard facts of the case. "Keith?" I asked, "is there anything on that computer? Anything . . . bad?"

He looked at me sourly. "No."

"Have you been in touch with Amy?"

"In touch?"

"E-mail."

"No," Keith said.

"Because if you have, they'll find that out," I warned.

He laughed almost derisively. "They would already know that, Dad," he scoffed. "They took the computer from Mr. Giordano's house, remember?"

I realized that Keith could only have known that the police had taken a computer from Amy's house if he'd actually been following news reports of the investigation. That the police had taken the Giordanos' computer had been mentioned on the evening news the night of her disappearance, and appeared only once in print, a brief notation in the local paper. From the beginning, he'd feigned indifference, even boredom, with the police. But clearly he had been keeping an eye on what they were doing.

"I asked you a question," I said sharply.

"That's all you ever do," Keith shot back. "Ask me questions." His eyes glittered angrily. "Why don't you just get to the one question you really want to ask. Go ahead, Dad. Ask me."

My lips jerked into an angry frown. "Don't start that, Keith."

"Ask the question," Keith repeated insistently, offering it as a challenge. "We all know what it is." He laughed bitterly. "All right, I'll ask it." He cocked his head to the right, and switched to a low, exaggeratedly masculine, voice. "So, Keith, did you kidnap Amy Giordano?"

"Stop it," I said.

He continued in the same mock fatherly tone. "Did you take her someplace and fuck her?"

"That's enough," I said. "Go to your room."

He didn't move, save for his fingers, which instantly crushed the inventory "No, Dad, not until I ask the last question."

"Keith . . ."

He cocked his head back and pretended to suck on an imaginary pipe. "So, my boy, did you kill Amy Giordano?"

"Shut up!" I shouted.

He stared at me brokenly, his tone now soft, almost mournful. "You believed it from the very first, Dad." With that, he turned away and walked slowly up the stairs.

I looked at Meredith, noticed that her eyes were glistening. "Is he right, Eric?" she asked. "Did you believe it from the beginning?"

"No, I didn't," I told her. "Why would I?"

She turned my question over in her mind, working it silently until she found the answer. "Maybe because you don't like him," she whispered. "Oh, I know you love him. But maybe you don't like him. It's what people do in families, isn't it? They love people they don't like."

I heard footsteps on the stairs, then the front door closed loudly.

"He's going for one of those walks, I guess," I said.

Those walks—Peak's words soured in my mouth, sounding suspicious, vaguely ominous, as they had when I first heard them.

"He's just trying to deal with it the only way he can," Meredith told me. "Which is alone, I guess."

Keith was already at the end of the walkway, moving swiftly, shoulders hunched head down, as if against a heavy wind.

"We'll never be normal again," Meredith said quietly.

It was a dark pronouncement, and I refused to accept it.

"Of course, we will," I said. "All of this will go away once Amy Giordano is found."

She kept her eyes on Keith, watching intently as he mounted the small hill and moved on up toward the main road. "We have to help him, Eric."

"How?"

"Get someone for him to talk to."

I thought of all my first family must have held secret, of its legacy of drink, unhappiness, and an old man's bitter cackle. Anything seemed better than that. "What was the counselor's name?" I asked. "The one at the college?"

Meredith smiled softly. "Rodenberry," she said. "He'll be at the party tomorrow."

FIFTEEN

Dr. Mays lived in an old sea-captain's house only a few blocks from the home in which I'd grown up and which had seemed happy to me, at least until Jenny's death. After that my mother had sunk into a deep gloom, while my father's financial losses grew more and more severe, so that within the year the house itself had gone on the block. But none of that dreary history returned to me as we swept past the old house that evening. Instead, it was my father's dismissive outburst that played upon my mind—*You have no idea.*

He'd said it as an accusation but adamantly refused to clarify what he meant. Perhaps, I thought, my father was merely grasping for attention, his undefined charge against my mother was only his way of asserting himself when faced by her hallowed memory. If this were true, he'd chosen a crude method of gaining ground. But he'd always been reckless with his words, prone to vicious insult, and so it was perfectly in character for him to lift himself by bringing my mother down. And yet, for all that, I couldn't help wondering what he'd meant in saying that my mother hadn't been devoted to him. I'd seen nothing but devotion—patient and abiding. She had overlooked all his faults, stood by his side as his little empire shrank and finally disappeared. She had defended him no matter how outrageous his actions or negligent his fatherhood. How could it be that through all those years I'd had no idea of her?

"We'll just act normal," Meredith said as I pulled the car up in front of Dr. Mays's house.

I offered a quick smile. "We are normal," I reminded her. "We don't have to act."

She seemed hardly to hear me. Her gaze was fixed on the house, the guests she could see milling about inside, her expression intense and oddly searching, like a woman on a widow's walk, peering out into the empty sea, hoping for the first fluttering glimpse of her husband's returning ship.

"What is it, Meredith?" I asked.

She turned toward me abruptly, as if I'd caught her unawares. "I just hope he's here," she said. "Stuart." She seemed to catch something odd in my expression. "So we can talk to him about Keith," she explained. "We *are* going to do that, aren't we? That's what we decided."

"Yes."

Dr. Mays greeted us at the door. He was a short bald man, with wire spectacles.

"Ah, Meredith," he said as he pumped her hand, then looked at me. "Hello, Eric."

We shook hands, and he ushered us into a spacious living room where several professors stood with their wives and husbands, sipping wine and munching little squares of cheese. We all stood by the fireplace for a time, exchanging the usual pleasantries. Then Meredith excused herself and drifted away, leaving me alone with Dr. Mays.

"You have a terrific wife, Eric," he said, his eyes on Meredith as she approached a tall man in a tweed jacket who stood beside a thin woman with straight black hair.

"We feel very fortunate to have her with us," Dr. Mays added.

I nodded. "She loves teaching."

"That's good to hear," Dr. Mays said. He plucked a celery stalk from a plate of assorted cut vegetables and dipped it in the small bowl of onion dip that rested on the table beside him. "I hope she doesn't find me stodgy."

Across the room, Meredith laughed lightly and touched the man's arm.

"Not at all," I said. "She's always telling me some joke or story you've told."

Dr. Mays appeared surprised. "Really?"

I laughed. "She loved the one about Lenny Bruce."

He looked at me quizzically. "Lenny Bruce?"

"The one about the difference between men and women," I said.

Dr. Mays shrugged. "I'm afraid I don't know that one."

"You know, the plateglass window."

Dr. Mays stared at me blankly. "She must have heard that from someone else," he said.

There was another burst of laughter from across the room. I looked over to see Meredith with her hand at her mouth, the way she always held it when she laughed, her eyes bright and strangely joyful, so different from the way she'd been only a few minutes before. The man in the tweed jacket laughed with her, but the woman beside him only smiled quietly, then took a quick sip from her glass.

"Who are they?" I asked. "The people with Meredith."

Dr. Mays looked over at them. "Oh, that's Dr. Rodenberry and his wife, Judith," he said. "He's our college counselor."

"Oh, yes," I said. "Meredith has mentioned him."

"Brilliant man," Dr. Mays said. "And very funny."

He gave me a few more details about Rodenberry, that he'd been at the college for five years, turned a moribund counseling service into a vibrant school function. After that, Dr. Mays said he had to mingle and stepped over to another group of teachers.

I took the opportunity to make my way across the room, where Meredith still stood, talking to the Rodenberrys.

She glanced over as I approached her.

"Hi," I said softly.

"Hi," Meredith said. She turned to Rodenberry and his wife. "Stuart, Judith, this is my husband, Eric."

I shook hands with the two of them, smiling as warmly as I knew how. Then there was a moment of awkward silence, eyes shifting about, Rodenberry's back and forth between me and Meredith, his wife's eyes darting toward me, then quickly away.

"I've mentioned this situation with Keith to Stuart," she said.

I looked at Rodenberry. "What do you think?" I asked.

He considered the question briefly. "Well, Keith's certainly under a lot of pressure."

That seemed hardly an answer, so I dug deeper.

"But do you think he needs professional help?" I asked.

Again Rodenberry appeared reluctant to answer directly. "Perhaps, but only if he's willing to accept it. Otherwise, counseling would just add to the pressure he's already under."

"So how can we tell?" I asked. "If he needs help, I mean."

Rodenberry glanced at Meredith in what appeared a signal for her to jump in.

"Stuart feels that we should raise the subject with Keith," she said. "Not present it to him as something we think he should do, but only raise it as a possibility."

"And see how he reacts," Rodenberry added quickly. "Whether he's immediately hostile, or if he seems amenable to the idea."

"And if he seems amenable?" I asked.

Again, Rodenberry's gaze slid over to Meredith. "Well, as I told Meredith," he said, now returning his attention to me, "I'd be more than happy to provide whatever help I can."

I started to add some final remark on the subject, but Rodenberry's wife suddenly withdrew from our circle, her head turned decidedly away, as if shielding her face from view.

"Judith has been ill," Rodenberry said quietly once his wife was out of earshot. Again he looked at Meredith, and in response she offered a smile that struck me as unexpectedly intimate, which Rodenberry immediately returned.

"Anyway," he said, now returning his gaze to me. "Let me know what you decide about Keith." He drew a card from his jacket pocket. "Meredith has my number at school," he said as he handed me the card, "but this is my private number. Call it anytime."

I thanked him, and after that Rodenberry walked across the room to join his wife beside a buffet table. Once there, he placed his arm on his wife's shoulder. She quickly stepped away, as if repulsed by his touch, so that Rodenberry's arm immediately fell free and dangled limply at his side.

"I think the Rodenberrys have problems," I said to Meredith.

She watched as Rodenberry poured himself a drink and stood alone beside the window, where Dr. Mays joined him a few minutes later.

"Dr. Mays didn't remember that Lenny Bruce remark," I said.

Meredith continued to stare straight ahead, which was odd for her, I realized, since her tendency was always to glance toward me when I spoke.

"The one about the plateglass window," I added.

Her eyes shot over to me. "What?"

"You didn't hear it from Dr. Mays," I repeated.

Meredith glanced back into the adjoining room. "Well, I heard it from somebody," she said absently.

"Maybe from Rodenberry," I suggested. "Dr. Mays says he's very funny."

"Yes, he is," Meredith said. Her eyes glittered briefly, then dimmed, as if a shadowy thought had skirted through her mind. "He'll be good with Keith" was all she said.

We left the party a couple of hours later, driving more or less silently back to our house. The light was on in Keith's room, but we didn't go up or call him or make any effort to find out if he was really there. Such surveillance would only have struck him as yet more proof that I thought him a criminal, and his mood had become far too volatile to incite any such added resentment.

And so we simply watched television for an hour, then went to bed. Meredith tried to read for a while, but before too long she slipped the book onto the floor beside the bed, then twisted away from me and promptly fell asleep.

But I couldn't sleep. I thought about Keith and Meredith, of course, but increasingly my thoughts returned me to my first family—Warren's story of the insurance man with the odd questions, the strange remark my father had made, his bitter assertion that I had no idea about my mother.

Could that be true? I wondered. Could it be true that I had never known my mother? Or my father? That Warren, for all our growing up together, remained essentially an enigma?

I got up, walked to the window, and peered out into the tangled, night-bound woods. In my mind, I saw the car that had brought Keith home that night, its phantom driver behind the wheel, a figure who suddenly seemed to me no less mysterious than my son, my wife, my father and mother and brother, mere shadows, dark and indefinable.

"Eric?"

It was Meredith's voice.

I turned toward the bed but couldn't see her there.

"Something wrong?"

"No, nothing," I told her, grateful that I hadn't turned on the light, since, had she seen me, she would have known it was a lie.

SIXTEEN

Leo Brock called me at the shop at eleven the next morning. "Quick question," he said. "Does Keith smoke?"

He heard my answer in the strain of a pause.

"Okay," he said, "What brand does he smoke?"

I saw the face of the pack as Keith snatched it from his shirt pocket. "Marlboro," I said.

Leo drew in a long breath. "And he told police that he never left the house, isn't that right?"

"Yes."

"For any reason."

"He said he never left the house," I told him. "What's happening, Leo?"

"My source tells me that the cops found four cigarette butts outside the Giordanos' house," Leo said. "Marlboro."

"Is that so bad?" I asked. "I mean, so what if Keith went out for a smoke?"

"They were at the side of the house," Leo added. "Just beneath Amy's bedroom window."

"Jesus," I breathed.

In my mind I saw Keith at the window, peering through the curtains of Amy's window, watching as she slept, her long dark hair splayed out across her pillow. Had he watched her undress, too? I wondered. And while doing that . . . done what? Had he gone to the water tower in search of similar stimulation? Before that moment, I would probably have avoided such questions, but something in my mind had hardened, taken on the shape of a pick or a spade, prepared to dig.

"So they think he was watching her," I said.

"We can't be sure what they're thinking."

"Oh come on, Leo, why would his cigarettes be there, at her window?"

"Not his," Leo cautioned. "Just the brand he smokes."

"Don't talk to me like a lawyer, Leo," I said. "This is bad and you know it."

"It doesn't help things," Leo admitted.

"They're going to arrest him, aren't they?"

"Not yet," Leo said.

"Why not?" I asked. "We both know they think he did it."

"First of all, no one knows what was done," Leo reminded me. "Remember that, Eric. Whatever the police may be thinking, they don't know anything. And there's something else to keep in mind. Keith didn't have a car. So how could he have taken Amy from her house?"

I made no argument to this, but I felt the water around me rise slightly.

"Eric?"

"Yes."

"You have to have faith."

I said nothing.

"And I don't mean that in a religious way," Leo added. "You have to have faith in Keith."

"Of course," I said quietly.

There was a pause, then Leo said, "One final . . . difficulty."

I didn't bother to ask what it was, but only because I knew Leo was about to tell me.

"Keith ordered a pizza for dinner that night," Leo said. "The pizza guy delivered it at just after eight. He said that when he arrived, he didn't see Amy, but Keith was there, and he was on the phone."

"The phone?"

"Did he call you that night?"

"Yes."

"When did he call?"

"Just before ten."

"Not before?"

"No."

"You're sure about that," Leo said. "You're sure that Keith only called you once that night."

"Only once," I said. "At around ten."

"And that's when he told you he'd be late and that he wouldn't need a ride, correct?"

"Yes."

T

THOMAS H. COOK

"Because he had a ride?"

"No," I said. "He said that he could get a ride."

"But not that he had one?"

"No, not that he had one."

"Okay," Leo said.

"So who was he on the phone with?" I asked. "When the pizza guy was there."

"I'm sure the police have the number," Leo said. "So it won't be long before they tell us."

We talked a few minutes longer, Leo doing what he could to put the best light on things. Still, for all his effort, I could sense nothing but a spiraling down, a room closing in, slowly dwindling routes of escape.

"What happens," I asked finally, "if they never find Amy?"

"Well, it's awfully hard to convict when there's no body," Leo answered.

"I wasn't thinking of that," I told him. "I mean, Keith would have to live with it, wouldn't he? The suspicion that he killed her."

"Yes, he would," Leo answered. "And I admit, cases like that, without any definite resolution, they can be painful to all concerned."

"Corrosive," I said softly, almost to myself.

"Corrosive, yes," Leo said. "It's hard, when you can't get to the bottom of something."

I had never known how true that was before that moment, how little whiffs of doubt could darken and grow menacing, urge you forward relentlessly, fix you in a need to find out what really happened. "Otherwise your whole life is an un-solved mystery," I said.

"Yeah, it's just that bad," Leo said. "You become a cold-case file."

A cold-case file.

I remember thinking that that was precisely what I was becoming, and that for the rest of that day, as I dealt with customers, framed a few pictures, I felt a fierce urgency building in me, a need to know about Keith, the life he might have hidden from me, the terrible thing I could not keep myself from thinking that he might, indeed, have done.

Just before I closed, I called Meredith and told her what Leo Brock had earlier told me. I expected her to be irritated that I hadn't called before, accuse me once again of refusing to confront things, but instead she took the latest development without surprise, as if she'd been expecting it all along.

"I have to work late tonight," she said. Her voice struck me as oddly wistful, like a woman who'd once lived in a perfect world, known its beauty and contentment, a world that was no more and would never be again. "I should be home by eleven."

I was on my way to my car a few minutes later when I noticed Warren's truck parked outside Teddy's bar. I guessed that he was probably drinking earlier and earlier, his usual pattern before plunging into a full-blown binge. In the past, I'd never been able to prevent his periodic dives, and because of that I had more or less stopped trying. But suddenly, faced with my own family problems, I found that I could see his more clearly. The contempt my father had so relentlessly heaped upon him had stolen away any shred of self-confidence he might otherwise have grasped, then the tragedy of Jenny's death, and after that, my mother's fatal accident. Perhaps, I told myself, he was not so much one of life's pathetic losers, as simply a man who had lost a lot.

He was sitting in the back booth, his paint-spattered hands wrapped around a mug of beer.

"Hey, Bro," he said as I slid into the seat opposite him. He lifted the beer. "Want a frosty?"

I shook my head. "No, I don't have much time. Meredith's working late, so I have to get home, make dinner for Keith."

He took a sip of the beer. "So," he said. "How's tricks?"

I shrugged. "The same."

"And this thing with Keith?"

"I have the feeling the cops are focusing on him." I added no further details, and typically, Warren didn't ask.

Instead he said, "They jump to conclusions, the cops. It only takes some little thing." He laughed. "But, that's the way we all are, right? Obsessed."

"Why do you say that?"

"You know, the way some crazy idea won't stop nagging at a guy."

Warren often spoke of himself in the third person, as "a guy."

"What crazy idea is nagging at you, Warren?" I asked.

I thought it was probably something about Keith, but I was wrong.

"For some reason I keep thinking about Mom," Warren said. "You know, how upset she was toward the end."

"Well, why wouldn't she be?" I said. "She was losing her house."

"That wasn't it," Warren said. "She never liked that house."

"She never liked the house?"

"No, she hated it," Warren said. He took a sip of beer. "It was too big, she said, too much to take care of."

"I didn't know she felt that way," I said.

"The house was for Dad," Warren said. "Part of the show. He wanted it because it made people think he was a big important guy." He glanced away, then back to me. "You seen him lately?"

"I see him every Thursday."

Warren smiled. "Dutiful," he said. "You've always been dutiful with Dad."

He made duty sound oddly disreputable. "I don't want him to feel abandoned, if that's what you mean."

Warren took a hard pull on the beer. "I dropped in on him this morning," he said. He looked at me with a bitter grin. "He said he never wanted to see me again."

"What? Why?"

"Because of what I told you, that insurance guy."

"Dad doesn't want to see you again because of that?" I asked unbelievingly.

"Yup," Warren said, now trying to make light of it. "Funny world, huh, Eric?"

I waved my hand. "He'll get over it."

Warren shook his head adamantly. "No, he won't. Not this time. I really pissed him off."

"But it was nothing," I argued.

"Not to Dad," Warren said. "He got in a real lather about it."

I recalled the look on my father's face when I'd broached the same subject with him, and suddenly I realized that the part of me that wished to avoid things, the part Meredith had long recognized, was dead. My suspicion had begun with a subtle itch, but now it was a raging affliction, a thousand bleeding sores I couldn't stop digging at.

"What's he hiding, Warren?" I asked bluntly.

Warren's eyes fell toward his hands.

"Warren?"

He shrugged.

I leaned toward him. "You were there that summer," I said. "What happened?"

Warren looked up shyly. "Dad thought she did something," he said. "Mom." He glanced about as if to make sure no one else was listening. "Something with this other guy. You know what I mean."

"Mom?" I was astonished. "What other guy?"

Warren took a sip. "Jason Benefield. The family lawyer, remember? Used to come over with papers for this or that."

I recalled him as a tall, well-dressed, and very courtly man with a great shock of gray hair, handsome in the way of old boats, rugged, worn, but graceful.

"Do you think it was true, what Dad thought?" I asked.

"Maybe," Warren said. He saw the surprise in my face, how little I'd believed it possible that he noticed anything. "I'm not stupid, Eric," he said. "I can see things."

"What did you see exactly?"

"That Mom was . . . that she liked this guy," Warren answered. "And that he felt the same way about her." He finished the drink and waved for another. "At first I didn't know what to think about it, you know? Mom and this guy. But then I knew how Dad treated her, like she was nothing except when his cronies came over. And so I just thought, Well, okay, good for Mom, you know?"

Peg arrived with Warren's beer. He smiled at her, but she didn't smile back.

"Bitch, huh?" Warren muttered after she'd stepped away. "But then, they all are, right?" He gave a quick self-mocking laugh. "At least to me."

"What made Dad suspect her?"

Warren ran his fingers through what was left of his hair. "Somebody tipped him off."

"Who?"

He hesitated, and so I knew I wouldn't like the answer, but comfort no longer mattered to me. "Who?" I repeated sternly.

"Aunt Emma," Warren answered. He took a long drink, glanced into the dying foam, then looked at me. "She saw Mom and Jason together. I mean, not in a bad way. Like in bed, or something like that. Mom would never have done anything, you know, at home. But one day Aunt Emma came over to bring some tomatoes from her garden. She heard Mom and this guy talking." He shrugged. "You know, the way people talk when there's something between them. You don't have to hear the words."

"And Aunt Emma told Dad?"

Warren nodded, returned his gaze to the glass, remained silent for a moment, then looked up. "He beat the hell out of her, Eric. I knew it was coming, so I took off. When I got back, Dad was sitting in the living room, drinking. Mom was upstairs. She didn't come down until the next morning. That's when I saw what he'd done to her." He seemed to return to that grim day. "I got real upset. I wanted to hit him. Like he hit her. I wanted to beat the shit out of him." He shook his head. "But I didn't do anything. I didn't even mention it." His eyes glistened slightly. "I never had any nerve, Eric. All Dad had to do was look at me, and I crumbled."

I shook my head. "I had no idea about any of this."

Warren nodded. "You couldn't have done anything, anyway. Nobody could do anything with Dad. Besides, he was good to you."

"Yes, to me," I admitted. "But you had to—"

Warren waved his hand to silence me. "Oh, don't worry about me and Dad. Then or now. Hell, I don't care if I never see him again." He took a long pull on the beer, one that left no doubt that it was my father's anger that had hurled him off the wagon. "Water under the bridge."

Except that it wasn't. At least not for me.

"I keep thinking about things, Warren," I told him. "I know it's because of this thing with Keith. But I keep going back to our family, too."

Warren laughed. "Why bother? They were gone before you grew up. Mom. Jenny. You were still a kid when they died."

"But I don't want to be a kid anymore," I told him. "I want to know what you know. About everything."

"I told you what I know."

"Maybe there was more," I said.

"Like what?"

"Like that insurance man you told me about. Why would he have come around the house, asking questions about Mom and Dad?"

Warren shrugged. "Who knows?"

"Dad told me there was no insurance on Mom," I said.

"Then I guess there wasn't any insurance." He took a sip of beer. "Jesus, what difference does it make, anyway?"

"It makes a difference because I want to know."

"Know what?"

The words fell like stones from my mouth. "If he killed her."

Warren's eyes grew very still. "Jesus, Eric."

"Fucked with the car some way. The brakes."

"Dad didn't know anything about cars, Eric."

"So, you don't think—"

Warren laughed. "Of course not." He peered at me as if I were very small, a creature he couldn't quite bring into focus. "What's the matter with you? Dad kill Mom? Come on, Eric."

"How can you be so sure?"

Warren laughed again, but this time, mirthlessly. "Eric, this is nuts."

"How do you know?" I repeated.

"Jesus, Eric," Warren said. "This is weird."

"What if he killed her?" I asked.

Warren remained silent for a moment, his gaze downcast, as if studying the last small portion of beer that remained. Then he said, "What good would it do, even if you found out he did?"

"I don't know," I said. "But as it stands, everything seems like a lie."

"So?"

"I don't want to live like that."

He drained the last of the beer. "Eric, everybody lives like that." He grinned and the grim seriousness of our former discussion simply fell away from him. "Lighten up, Bro—everybody's fake."

I leaned forward and planted my elbows on the table. "I want to know the truth."

Warren shrugged lightly. "Okay, fine," he said wearily. "Knock yourself out. Hell, Dad's a pack rat. Kept everything in that old metal filing cabinet, remember? Wouldn't throw it away, or anything in it. Heavy fucking thing. Remember the trouble we had moving it into your basement?" He drained the last of the beer and looked at me drowsily. "If he had a policy on Mom," he said, "that's where it would be."

SEVENTEEN

The next night, after Meredith and Keith had already gone to bed, I quietly made my way to the basement. It was a gray metal filing cabinet, the one in which my father had kept his records and which Warren and I had removed from the little house my father had lived in before I'd finally convinced him to take up residence at the retirement home.

I'd taken him to Shelton Arms on a snowy January day, then returned to the house and helped Warren pack up Dad's belongings and transport them to the basement where they'd rested undisturbed until now.

My father's old rolltop desk stood beside the cabinet. I opened it, pulled over a plain metal chair, took out a stack of files from the top drawer of the cabinet, and began to go through the yellow crumbling papers I found inside, the records of my father's many failed enterprises along with his increasingly desperate attempts to salvage them.

But that was not the history I was looking for. I didn't care that my father had failed, that his business dealings were shadowy, that he'd squandered thousands of dollars to keep up appearances, joined expensive clubs at the very time my mother was scouring local thrift shops in order to keep her children clothed.

None of that mattered because I wasn't looking for evidence of bad business decisions or foolish investments. I was Peak and Kraus, my gaze, like theirs, focused by suspicion, looking for evidence of a crime.

It emerged slowly, like a body rising through layers of accumulated silt, the excruciating details of my father's ruin. The decline began in the late sixties as his real estate holdings were decimated by soaring interest rates. Steadily, for five years, he defaulted on one mortgage after another, his banker friends no longer willing to extend further credit, so that he lost both residential lots and commercial properties, his wealth dropping from him like petals from a wilting rose.

By the fall of 1974, he had nothing left but the family house, itself mortgaged to the gills, literally sinking in a slough of debt. I was twelve years old that autumn, now attending the expensive private school my father had denied Warren, a little boy dressed in his school uniform, complete with navy blue blazer with brass buttons, the crest of Saint Regis embroidered on the breast pocket.

Each night, I returned to a house that was disappearing, though I didn't know that at the time. Warren stayed in his room most of the time, and Jenny had begun complaining of terrible headaches. My mother made increasingly modest meals, which she served at a table my father hardly frequented anymore. "He's in New York," my mother would explain, "on business."

The disastrous nature of that business was apparent in the papers I rifled through that night, applications for loans and their subsequent denials, threatening letters from lawyers and creditors and even local tradesmen, all of them demanding payment . . . or else.

Under such a barrage, men have been driven to suicide or simply run away, in either case leaving their families to fend for themselves. But on rare occasions some men take a third, far more drastic, option. They kill their families.

Until that night, it had never occurred to me that at some desperate moment, with the fifth scotch of the evening trembling in his hand, my father might actually have considered this final course.

Then, suddenly, it was there, the terrifying suggestion that he had.

A suggestion, not evidence, and yet it stopped me cold, so that for a long time, I simply stared at what I'd stumbled upon, the real estate section of the *Los Angeles Times,* dated April 27, 1975, and wondered how this particular section of a paper from a city several thousand miles away had come into my father's hands, and why, halfway down column three, he had drawn a red circle around a particular advertisement, one offering a "neat, clean, studio . . . suitable for bachelor."

Suitable for bachelor.

In what way, I wondered, had my father planned to be a bachelor again?

Was it only that he'd considered option one, abandonment?

Or had he considered option three as well, a final, irrevocable break that would truly leave him free?

I didn't know, couldn't know, and yet, in my current state of mind, one the shadowy basement perfectly mirrored, I found that I could neither dismiss the possibility that my father had truly contemplated our murders nor suppress my need to discover if he actually had.

And so I continued through his papers, watching with an ever-deepening sense of desperation as his circumstances grew more dire. As the weeks of that last disastrous year passed, the dunning letters became more threatening and my father's responses increasingly laced with fabrications. He began to invent correspondence with "anonymous backers," to claim sources of revenue he did not have, and to pepper his letters with the names of important people—mostly politicians—who were, he said, "getting in on the ground floor" of whatever wholly fanciful enterprise he was at that moment proposing. The line between delusion and reality appeared to fade, and because of that, I could no longer tell if he was outright lying or if he had begun to believe his own fantasies.

Then, in yet another stack of business correspondence, this one interspersed with yellowing family photographs, I found a letter from my father's sister, Emma. It was dated February 3, 1975, a short two and a half months before my mother's death. One line in particular caught my attention:

"As you say, Edward, these current straits are due entirely to Margaret's outrageous spending."

My mother's outrageous spending? On what had my mother spent outrageously? I knew the answer all too well. She had spent "outrageously" on used clothes at the Catholic thrift shop, on bruised vegetables at the market. She'd spent on bent cans and day-old bread. Despite our dwindling resources, she had tried with all her might to keep her children decently clothed and fed. During the year of Jenny's death, she had bought absolutely nothing for herself. Not so much as a hat or an earring.

That my father could blame my mother for his own financial mismanagement was deplorable enough. But the line he'd scrawled in the margin beside my aunt's comment was worse: *"Now let her get me out of it."*

Me.

Not us.

So what exactly were we—his wife and three children— to my father, I wondered. The answer was implicit in his use of "me." We were nothing.

We were nothing, and so he could go to New York, pick up a copy of the *Los Angeles Times*, pull out the real estate section, peruse it casually on the train back to Wesley, circle an ad for a neat clean studio, "suitable for bachelor."

And how might he regain his bachelorhood?

The darkest possible scenario immediately unspooled in my mind: my father waiting until deep in the night, then moving silently downstairs to his office, opening the rolltop desk, unlocking a small wooden cubicle, and drawing out the pistol he had always kept there. The very pistol which, as if in some miraculous vision, glimmered darkly before me, still in the cubicle where he'd left it. Had he reached for it, as I now did, then taken it up the stairs to where his family slept, as my family also did, he would have been but three quick shots from freedom.

But if that had ever been his plan, why had he not done it? Others had. Men like my father, ruined in business, in dread of humiliation, men who'd lost everything, and so, on a cool evening had decided to start over in the most profound and devastating way a man can seek deliverance. They had methodically murdered their families. Why had my father refused to take that road? Why had he not even decided on the less awesome route of simply climbing on a plane or train or bus and vanishing into the night?

I knew that his remaining with us had nothing to do with love. My mother's power over him had faded with her beauty. He felt nothing but contempt for Warren. And Jenny, for whom he'd seemed to have a true affection, had only just died. That left me, and so, briefly, I entertained the notion that his hopes for me had provided the one force that held us together. He had, after all, sent me to the best school, and when he talked about my future, it was always in the brightest terms. I would go to an Ivy League college, become a powerhouse in some business or law firm. I would be the son he'd dreamed of, proof of his worth, as much an ornament as my mother's beauty had once been.

But by April 1975, even that dream was surely dying. There would be no money for an Ivy League education, as my father must have known, and without it how could I fulfill his vision of a rich, successful son?

For a moment, I considered my father's predicament. He was bankrupt, saddled with a family he cared little for, his daughter already dead.

Why then had he stayed with us?

The answer occurred to me instantly. He'd stayed because somewhere in the dark tangle of his business and family relations, he had found a way out.

The single line he'd written in the margin of his sister's letter now returned to me in a sinister whisper. *Now let her get me out of it.*

In a vision, I put myself in my brother Warren's place on that long ago summer afternoon. I am sitting on the grand staircase, reading a book. The doorbell rings. I answer it. A tall lean man in a dark suit draws a gray hat from his head and stares at me with small, quiet, sparklingly inquisitive eyes. His voice is calm, soothing, like Peak's: *No reason to be alarmed.* He is from the insurance company, he says, investigating something, that much is clear, though he doesn't tell me what he's looking into. And so I let him in, as Warren did, then go back to the stairs, my book. He leaves after a few minutes. He does not tell me what he was looking for, and the years go by and I marry and have a son and never ask him what he sought that day.

But now I know, and within only a few minutes it is in my hands, buried among other papers, but not deeply. Like a body hurriedly covered with leaves and fallen branches, the lightest digging brings it up, not a policy exactly, but a letter to my father, informing him that the life insurance policy on his wife has been approved in the amount of two hundred thousand dollars.

"Eric?"

I looked up and saw Meredith standing at the bottom of the stairs. I hadn't heard her come down them, the soft tread of her feet muffled by the stormy currents in my own mind.

"What are you doing down here?" she asked in a voice that seemed faintly alarmed, like she'd stumbled upon some oddity in me that called other, once-stable, characteristics into question.

"Just going through some old stuff," I answered.

She peered at the pile of papers that lay strewn across the desk. "What are you looking for?"

I quickly glanced down and noticed a photograph. "This," I said, lifting it from the pile for her to see.

It was a family photograph, the last one taken of all of us together. My father and mother on the front steps of the big house, their three children lined up in front of them, Warren on the left, Jenny on the right, me in the middle.

Who had I been then? I wondered as I glanced at the picture. How much had I known that year? How much had I refused to know? And not just about hidden things, the insurance policy, my mother's grief, but about the most obvious aspects of life in the big house. Had I once considered how cruelly Warren was treated or that Jenny sometimes had headaches and fell for no reason at all, or that my mother often sat silently at the kitchen table, toying distractedly with a crushed napkin? Had I once glanced out the window of the fancy bus that whisked me to Saint Regis each morning, looked out as the big house grew small in the distance, and allowed myself to confront the possibility that something might be wrong?

I looked at my wife, noted the wariness in her gaze, and Leo Brock's words sounded in my mind, the disturbing intimation that all was not well in my own house, either, and that someone out there knew it.

Something wrong.

For a moment, I imagined the source of that discomforting remark, saw a phantom person pawing through my papers as I'd just pawed through my father's, full of suspicion but with no real evidence. I suddenly felt an annihilating fury at whomever it was who'd phoned the police hotline, a rage that was not in the least calmed by the fact that I could not even be sure that there was such a person. And yet I believed that there was, believed it so powerfully that I instantly imagined the caller's voice as something between a lascivious whisper and the hissing of a snake. The caller's profile emerged no less fully formed—a fat puffy face, with thick moist lips and a day's growth of facial hair. I could even see the outline of his room, dirty and disheveled, littered with grease-stained paper napkins and empty pizza boxes. He was a bachelor, this man, lonely and hateful, someone who'd seen either me or Meredith or Keith and fixed some sullen and resentful part of himself upon us. He had created histories for us, I decided, and ran those histories through his mind, sneering at a family whose imagined perfection he despised.

"You don't want me to see it?"

I came out of my reverie to find Meredith now at the desk, tugging at a picture I had reflexively resisted letting go.

"Of course, you can see it," I said. I released the photograph and watched as Meredith gazed at it expressionlessly.

"Why were you looking for this particular picture?" Meredith asked.

I shrugged. "I don't know," I said. "Maybe because it was the last time everything seemed"—the final word cracked something deep within me—"right."

She handed the picture back to me. "Are you going to stay down here all night?"

I shook my head. "No," I told her. "Just a little longer."

She turned and headed back up the stairs, head bent forward slightly, her hair dangling in dark waves on the side of her face. At the top of the stairs, she stopped and stood on the landing. For a moment, I thought she might come back down to me, take a deep breath and—

Confess?

I stared at her, stunned by the word that had suddenly popped into my mind. What had Meredith done that required confession? And yet, there it was, the idea thrown up from some murky depth inside me, suspicion now flowing into empty space, filling it with a sharp, acrid smoke, so that I felt trapped in a furiously overheated room, flames licking at me from all directions, with no way to douse the ever-rising fire.

EIGHTEEN

Monday morning I got up early, walked to the kitchen and made coffee. For a long time I sat alone at the small oval table that overlooked the front yard. I recalled the previous night's search through my father's papers, the incriminating documents I'd found among them, and felt again a searing need to get to the bottom of what, if anything, had actually happened to my mother. At the same time I knew nowhere to go with what I'd found. I recalled how Meredith had come down to the basement, the strange accusation my mind had seized upon, the licking flames that had suddenly sprung up all around me, which I now laid at the feet of the undeniable strain I'd been under since Amy Giordano's disappearance. It was this tension that had created the false fires I felt still burning in me, I decided, fires which, when the mystery of her circumstances was finally resolved, would surely weaken and gutter out.

Keith came down the stairs at just past seven. He didn't bother to come into the kitchen. He'd never been hungry in the morning, and neither Meredith nor I any longer insisted that he eat something before going to school. And so on this particular morning, like most others, he simply swept down the stairs and out the door to where his bike lay on its side in the dewy grass, mounted it, and peddled away.

He'd already disappeared up the hill when Meredith came into the kitchen. Normally by this time she would be fully dressed for work, so it surprised me that she was still in her housecoat, the belt drawn tight, her feet bare, hair in disarray. She hadn't put on the usual light coat of makeup either, and I noticed dark circles under her eyes. She looked tense and un-rested, worn down by what we'd been going through.

"I'm not going in to work today," she said. She poured a cup of coffee, but instead of joining me at the table, walked to the window and stared out into the yard.

Her back was to me, and I admired her shape, the way she'd so carefully maintained it. She had broad shoulders, and long sleek legs, and despite her drawn appearance, I knew why men still turned when she came into the room.

"Keith's already gone," I told her.

"Yeah, I saw him out the window." She took a sip of cof-fee and kept her eyes fixed on the front yard. "I'll just call it a personal day," she said. "They don't ask questions when you take a personal day."

I walked over to her, wrapped my arms loosely around her

shoulders. "Maybe I'll take off, too. Go to a movie or some-thing. Spend the whole day. Just the two of us."

She shook her head and pulled out of my arms. "No, I have to work. It's not that kind of personal day."

"What work?" I asked.

"I need to write a lecture. On Browning."

"I thought you'd written all your lectures. Wasn't that what all those late nights at the library were about?"

She returned to the coffee machine. "All but Browning," she said. "I have the notes here."

"Any chance of finishing it by afternoon? We could go for a long walk together."

"No, I won't be finished by then," she answered. She came over to me and pressed an open palm against the side of my face. "But I'll cook a nice dinner. French. With candles. Wine." She smiled thinly. "We might even persuade Keith to join us."

I drew her hand away and held it lightly. "What about Rodenberry?"

Her eyes tensed.

"Are we going to talk to Keith about him?"

My question seemed to put her at ease. "I think we should," she said.

"All right."

I left her, walked upstairs, and finished dressing. She was sitting at the kitchen table, sipping from her cup, when I came back down.

She smiled when she saw me. "Have a nice day," she said.

———

Detective Peak was waiting for me when I arrived at the shop. This time he was dressed casually, in a light flannel jacket and open-collar shirt. As I came toward him, he edged away from the side of the building and nodded.

"I wonder if we could have a cup of coffee," he asked.

"I've already had my morning coffee," I answered coolly.

"Just one cup," Peak said, but not in the distant professional tone he'd used with Meredith. Instead, there was now something unexpectedly fraternal in his manner, as if we were old war buddies and so could talk to each other in full trust and confidence.

"You'll be able to open on time," he added.

"All right," I said with a shrug.

We walked to the diner at the end of the block. It was owned by the Richardsons, a couple who'd moved to Wesley from New York only a few years before. They'd shunned the sleek art deco look of city diners and tried for a homey design instead, wooden tables, lace curtains, porcelain salt and pepper shakers in the form of a nineteenth-century sea captain and his wife. Before that morning, I'd hardly noticed the décor, but now it struck me as false and unnatural, like a bad face-lift.

"Two coffees," Peak said to Matt Richardson as we took a table near the front window.

Peak smiled. "May I call you Eric?"

"No."

The smiled vanished. "I have a family, too," he said. He waited for me to respond. When I didn't, he folded his arms on the table and leaned into them. "It's my day off," he added.

I immediately suspected that this was Peak's new approach and that it was meant to soften me up, a way of telling me that he'd taken a special interest in the case, was trying to be of help. A week before, I might have believed him, but now I thought it just an act, something he'd learned at police interrogation school.

The coffees came. I took a quick sip, but Peak left his untouched.

"This doesn't have to go any further," he said. His voice was low, measured. It conveyed a sense of guarded discretion. "Absolutely no further."

He drew in a deep preparatory breath, like a man about to take a long dive into uncertain waters. "We found things on Keith's computer."

My hands trembled very slightly, like shaking leaves. I quickly dropped them into my lap and put on a stiff unflappable face.

"What did you find?" I asked.

Peak's face was a melancholy mask. "Pictures."

"Pictures of what?" I asked stonily.

"Children."

The earth stopped turning.

"They aren't illegal, these pictures," Peak added quickly. "They're not exactly child pornography."

"What are they?"

He looked at me pointedly. "You're sure you don't know anything about these pictures?"

"No, nothing."

"You never use Keith's computer?"

I shook my head.

"Then the pictures have to be Keith's," Peak said. He made a show of being genuinely sorry that the pictures had turned up. Part of his new act, I decided, his effort to suggest that he'd come to me in search of an explanation, one that would get Keith off the hook. I had a photo shop, after all. Maybe I was interested in "art pictures." If so, as he'd already assured me, nothing would go further.

"The children are all girls," Peak continued. "They look to be around eight years old." He bit his lower lip, then said. "Nude."

I felt the only safety lay in silence, so I said nothing.

"We've talked to Keith's teachers," Peak said. "He seems to have self-esteem problems."

I saw Keith in my mind, the limp drag of his hair, how unkempt he was, the slouch of his shoulders, the drowsy, listless eyes. Was that the posture of his inner view of himself, hunched, sloppy, worthless?

"Low self-esteem is part of the profile," Peak said.

I remained silent, afraid the slightest word might be used against my son, quoted by the prosecution, used to buttress the case, contribute to conviction.

"Of men who like children," Peak added.

I clung to silence like the shattered bow of a sinking boat, the only thing that could keep me afloat in the rising water.

"Do you want to see the pictures?" Peak asked.

I didn't know what to do, couldn't figure out Peak's scheme. If I said no, what would that mean? And if I said yes, what would he gather from that?

"Mr. Moore?"

I raced to figure out the right answer, then simply tossed a mental coin.

"I guess I should," I said.

He had them in his car, and as I made my way across the parking lot, I felt like a man following the hangman to the waiting gallows.

Peak got in behind the wheel. I took my place on the passenger side. He picked up the plain manila folder that rested on the seat between us. "We printed these off Keith's computer. As I said, they're not illegal. But I'm sure you can understand that they're a problem for us, something we can't ignore."

I took the envelope and drew out the pictures. The stack was about half an inch thick, twenty, maybe thirty photographs. One by one, I went through them, and just as Peak said, they weren't exactly pornographic. All of the girls were posed alone in natural settings, never indoors, little girls in bright sunlight, their tiny budding breasts barely detectible on their gleaming white chests. Naked, they sat on fallen trees or beside glittering streams. They were sometimes shot from the front, sometimes from the rear, sometimes their whole bodies in profile, standing erect, or sitting, knees to their chins, their arms enfolding their legs. They had long hair and perfectly proportioned bodies. They were beautiful in the flawless, innocent way of childhood beauty. None, I guessed, was more than four feet tall. None had pubic hair. All of them were smiling.

So what do you do at such a moment? As a father. What do you do after you've looked at such pictures, then returned them to the manila envelope, and lowered the envelope back down upon the car seat?

You do this. You look into the closely regarding eyes of another man, one who clearly thinks your son is, at best, a pervert, and at worse, a kidnapper, perhaps a rapist, a murderer. You look into those eyes and because you have no answer to the terrible accusation you see in them, you say simply, "What about his room? Did you find anything?"

"You mean, magazines . . . things like that?" Peak asked. "No, we didn't."

I hazarded another question. "Anything connected to Amy?"

Peak shook his head.

"So where are we?"

"We're still investigating," Peak said.

I looked at him evenly. "What did you hope to get by showing me those pictures?"

"Mr. Moore," Peak said evenly, "in a case like this, it always goes better if we can stop the investigation."

"Stop it with a confession, you mean," I said.

"If Keith voluntarily gives us a statement, we can help him," Peak said. He studied my face for a moment. "The Giordanos want their daughter back. They want to know where she is, and they want to bring her home." He drew the envelope up against the side of his leg. "And, of course, they want to know what happened to her," he added. "If it were your child, you'd want that, too, I'm sure."

He was into the depths of his kinder, gentler ruse, but I'd

had enough. "I assume we're done," I said sharply, then reached for the handle of the door. Peak's voice stopped me dead.

"Has Keith ever mentioned a man named Delmot Price?" Peak asked.

I recognized the name. "He owns the Village Florist Shop. Keith delivers there sometimes."

"And that's all you know about them?"

"Them?" I asked.

"We traced the call," Peak said. "I'm sure your lawyer has told you about it. The one the pizza deliveryman saw Keith making at the Giordanos'. It was placed to Delmot Price."

I started to speak, then stopped and waited.

"He knows Keith quite well," Peak added significantly.

I saw the car draw into the driveway as it had that night, its twin beams sweeping through the undergrowth, then Keith as he made his way down the unpaved road, brushed past the Japanese maple, and came into the house.

"Were they together that night?" I asked.

"Together?"

"Keith and Delmot Price."

"What makes you think they were together?" Peak asked.

I couldn't answer.

"Mr. Moore?"

I shook my head. "Nothing," I said. "Nothing makes me think they were together."

Peak saw the wound open up in me. I was a deer and he was an archer who knew he'd aimed well. I could almost feel the arrow dangling from my side.

"Did you know Keith had a relationship with this man?" Peak asked.

"Is that what he has?"

"According to Price, it's sort of a father-son thing."

"Keith has a father," I said sharply.

"Of course," Peak said softly, "but he talks to Price, you know, about himself, his problems. That he's not happy. Feels isolated."

"You think I don't know that about him?"

Peak seemed to be peering into my brain, looking through its many chambers, searching for the clue to me.

"I'm sure of one thing," he said. "You want to help Keith. We all want to help Keith."

It was all I could do to keep from laughing in Peak's face because I knew it was an act, scripted, a carefully laid trap to get me to incriminate my son; Peak had been moving at just the right pace, dropping little bits of information, then holding back, waiting. Which he was doing now, his eyes very still until he blinked slowly, released a small sigh, then said, "Did you know that Keith steals?"

I drew in a quick breath but did not reply.

"Price caught him stealing money from the cash register in his shop," Peak said. "Keith begged him not to say anything, and that's how they started talking."

I pretended to scoff at the outrageous nature of this latest charge. "That's ridiculous," I said. "Keith has everything he needs. And in addition, I pay him for the work he does at the shop."

"Not enough evidently."

"He has everything he needs," I insisted. "Why would he steal?"

Again, Peak waited for just the right amount of time before releasing his next arrow. "According to Price, he's trying to get enough money to run away."

"Run away? To where?"

"Anywhere, I guess."

Meaning, anywhere as long as it was away from me, from Meredith, from the burden of our family life.

"When was he going to do it?" I asked icily.

"As soon as he got enough money, I suppose." Peak leaned back and raked the side of his face.

"Unless this whole thing about Keith stealing isn't true," I said quickly. "Have you thought of that? Maybe Price is lying. Maybe Keith never took anything."

"Maybe," Peak said. "Why don't you ask him?"

He was setting me up, and I knew it. He was setting me up to do his work for him, interrogate my son.

"What have you asked him, Mr. Moore?" Peak said. "Have you asked him directly if he hurt Amy Giordano?"

He saw the answer in my eyes.

"Have you asked him anything about that night?"

"Of course, I have."

"What?"

"Well, for one thing, I asked him if he had any reason to think that Amy might have run away," I said. "Or if he'd seen anything suspicious around her house. A prowler, something like that."

"And he said no, right?"

I nodded.

"And you believed him, of course," Peak said. "Any father would." He leaned toward me slightly. "But Keith's not exactly who you think he is," he said gravely.

It was all I could do not to sneer. "Yeah, well," I said, "who is?"

NINETEEN

Yeah, well, who is?

I had never said anything so disturbing, and for the rest of the morning, as it echoed in my mind, I recalled similar sentiments I'd heard of late: Meredith's *Because people lie, Eric;* Warren's *Everybody's fake.* That I would remember such painful statements didn't strike me as particularly unusual. What was incontestably alarming was that this time I'd made such a statement myself. Why? I couldn't find an answer. All I knew was that each time I tried to think it through, examine the tortuous changes I could feel in myself, I returned to a single gnawing memory. Again and again, like a loop of film continually unfolding the same image, I saw Jenny that last time, mute, dying, her eyes full of a terrible urgency as she pressed her lips to my ear. Clearly she had been struggling against all odds to tell me something. In the years since her death I'd imagined it as some great truth she'd glimpsed on the precipice of death. But now, I wondered if that urgent communication might have been no more than some similarly dreary truth: *Don't trust anyone or anything—ever.*

I thought of Keith, the way I'd found him smoking sullenly near the playground, then of the things Peak had told me, that he had "a father-son thing" with Delmot Price and that he was a thief and planned to run away. All of this had come as a complete surprise, facts, if they were facts, which I couldn't have guessed, and which, if true, pointed to the single unavoidable truth that I did not know my son.

Suddenly, out of nowhere, a boiling wave of anger washed over me, anger at myself. What kind of father was I, really, if Keith had found it necessary to find another man, confide in him, reveal his most secret plans?

I had always felt terribly superior to my own father, far more involved with my son than he had ever been with any of his children. Even during Jenny's last days he'd made overnight business trips to Boston and New York, assigning Warren to stay at her bedside, see her through the night, a job my brother had made no effort to avoid, save on that last night, as I recalled now, when he'd emerged from Jenny's room looking old and haggard, a boy who, from his pale, stricken appearance on that gloomy morning, looked as if he'd seen the worst of things.

But now I wondered if, in fact, I was any better at fatherhood than my own father had been. When was the last time I'd actually talked with my son? Sure, we chatted over dinner, exchanged hasty asides as we passed each other in the hallway. But that was not real talk. Real talk bore the weight of hopes and dreams, tore away facades, and let each face shine in revealing light. Real talk was about life, the way we try to get through it, make the best of it, what we learn along the way. This kind of talk Keith had saved for Delmot Price, the man he'd gone to because he could not come to me, and who, if I were to begin to get a handle on my son before it was too late, I knew I would have to seek out, too.

Delmot Price wasn't hard to find, and the moment he saw me come through the door of his flower shop, he looked like a man who'd suddenly found himself in the crosshairs of a rifle scope.

He'd been wrapping a dozen long-stem red roses as I came into the shop. I stood off to the side and waited while he completed the task, took payment, and with a quick smile, thanked the woman whose roses they were.

During that time, I noted how gracefully he moved, his white hair gleaming in the overhead light, his long fingers folding the silver foil just so, tying the gold ribbon with a perfect knot. His fingers moved like dancers in a flowing and oddly beautiful choreography. There was no room for the slightest misstep, they had that kind of precision. And so it was obvious that in Keith, Price had not found a boy who was like himself, the way an English teacher might find a student with the same literary aspirations the teacher had once known as a youth. But instead, Delmot Price had found his opposite in Keith, a graceless, slovenly boy with tangled hair and a sullen smirk, a boy he'd befriended not out of admiration but because he pitied my son, felt sorry for how awkward and isolated and utterly directionless he was, how in need, as Price must have supposed, of a father.

He came toward me like a man wending his way out of a perfumed garden, weaving through swollen buds and broad-petaled flowers.

"Mr. Moore," he said. He started to offer his hand, then stopped, unsure if I'd take it.

And so I offered mine.

"I don't mean to intrude," I said.

He nodded, stepped to the door, turned the OPEN sign to CLOSED, and ushered me to the rear of the shop where we stood discreetly hidden behind a wall of ferns.

"The police talked to me," he said. "I suppose you know that."

"Yes."

"Just so you know, I don't believe Keith had anything to do with the disappearance of that little girl."

"I don't, either," I said, then realized that in part this was a lie, and so, I added, "but he's done troubling things. He stole from you."

Price nodded softly.

"Why does he want to run away?" I asked.

Price hesitated, like a doctor just asked how long a precious relative actually has to live. "He's not happy, Mr. Moore."

"Can you be more specific?"

I could see him working toward an answer, searching through a lifetime of words, images, experiences, looking for just the right one.

"Let me put it this way," Price said at last. "I have a greenhouse at my home, and most of the time, when I order a particular seed, it comes just the way it's supposed to. If I order a rose, I get a rose. But once in a while, I get something I didn't order, maybe don't even like. Geranium, something like that. I plant the seed, hoping for a rose, and up comes a geranium. At that point, I have to change the plan. I can't feed it and water it like I would if it were the rose I'd hoped for. I have to say, Okay, it's a geranium. It'll never be a rose. But at least I can raise it to be a healthy geranium. See what I mean? I have to adjust, because I didn't get what I ordered."

"Keith thinks I want a different son?" I asked.

"No," Price said. "He knows you do."

"Okay, but what good would running away do?" I asked.

"None, probably," Price said. "Which is what I told him. 'No matter where you go,' I said, 'it goes with you.'"

"What goes with him?"

"Your low opinion of him."

He saw that he'd delivered a stomach-emptying blow.

"I had the same problem with my son," he said quickly.

"Did he run away?" I asked.

Price's eyes glistened suddenly. "No," he said. "He killed himself."

A vision of Keith doing the same shot through my mind. I saw him in his room, opening the Swiss Army knife I'd given him for his thirteenth birthday, sliding its now-rusty blade across his pale wrists, watching as the crimson stream flowed down his arms and puddled between his bare feet, watching it dully, merely waiting for the final sleep to come upon him, his face expressionless, indifferent to the worthless life he was ending, doing all of this with an utterly flat affect.

"I'm sorry," I whispered.

"I was like a lot of fathers, I had great plans for my son," Price told me. "The trouble is, they weren't *his* plans."

"What are Keith's plans, did he tell you?"

Price shrugged. "I'm not sure he has any. Except this idea of getting away."

"He can't do that now," I said. "Not after Amy. He has to know that."

"I'm sure you've made it clear."

I realized that I'd done no such thing, and that the reason I'd not done it was no more complicated than the fact that I simply didn't like talking to Keith, seeing his dead, dull eye peering at me through the slit of his open door. The weight of the truth hit me like a hammer—the fact was, my son simply and undeniably repulsed me. I hated the way he slumped around, the tangle of his hair, the listlessness that over-whelmed him, the sheer dull thud of him. I hated all that, but had tirelessly labored to give no sign of it. Instead I had cheered his every modest achievement, praised and pho-tographed his ridiculously infantile science project, patted him on the back so often and with such false force that my hand had grown numb with the practice. I had worked hard to conceal what I really thought, and I had failed utterly. For all his seeming obliviousness, Keith had seen through me, di-vined and suffered silently the full depth of my contempt.

Price touched my arm. "It's not your fault, the way Keith feels," he assured me. "I can see how much you love him."

"Yes, of course," I said, then shook hands, said good-bye, turned, and walked through the scented air with my wife's words echoing in my head—*Everybody lies.*

Meredith was on the phone when I arrived at the house a few minutes later. I heard her voice as I opened the door, no doubt surprising her, since it was still early in the day and I wasn't expected back until the end of it.

"Gotta go" I heard her say, then the snap of her cell phone closing shut. She'd sunk it into the pocket of her housecoat by the time she greeted me.

"Oh, hi," she said as she walked out of the kitchen. She smiled. "I was just making another pot of coffee."

On the counter behind her, I noted the coffee machine sitting idly, the first morning pot still half full.

"You're getting to be a purist, I guess," I told her.

She looked at me quizzically.

"A coffee purist," I explained. "Never drink coffee that was brewed more than two hours before."

She laughed, but tensely. "Oh," she said, "is that the rule for coffee snobs?" She tossed her hair. "Where do you hear things like that, Eric?"

"Television, I guess."

For a moment, we faced each other silently. Then Meredith said, "So, what are you doing home so early?"

"Peak was waiting for me when I got to work," I told her.

Suddenly she paled. "The hotline," she blurted. "Someone's spreading—"

I shook my head. "No. This is not about the hotline. They found out a few things about Keith. Things we have to talk about."

I turned, walked into the living room, and sat down on the sofa.

Meredith trailed behind and took the chair opposite me.

"Peak told me two things," I began. "That Keith has been talking to someone. Delmot Price. He owns the Village Flower Shop. Anyway, Price caught Keith stealing from him. They started talking about it. Keith told him that he was stealing because he needed money."

"Needed money?" Meredith asked.

"To run away," I added grimly. "That's why he was stealing."

She was silent for a long time, like someone hit between the eyes, dazed, groping to regain her balance.

"Peak talked to his teachers, too," I added. "They say he has a problem with low self-esteem." The last piece of information was the hardest, but I had no choice but to deliver it. "That's part of the profile, he says . . . of a child molester."

Her eyes began to dart around, as if the air was filled with tiny explosions. "The car," she said tensely. "Do you think it was Price?"

"No," I said. "I talked to him right after Peak left. He's a good man, Meredith. He had a son like Keith."

"What do you mean, like Keith?"

"A kid with this problem, you know, esteem," I said. "Only worse. He killed himself."

Meredith's lips parted wordlessly.

"Price was just trying to help Keith," I said. "A shoulder to cry on, that's all."

Meredith shook her head slowly.

"It gets worse, Meredith. They found some pictures on Keith's computer. Little girls. Naked."

Meredith's right hand lifted to her closed lips.

"Not pornography exactly," I added. "But bad enough."

She stood up. "This is terrible," she whispered.

"Keith can't run away," I told her. "We have to make sure of that. No matter what he was planning before, he can't do it now. The police would think he was running away from this thing with Amy. They would never believe that—" I stopped because for a moment the words were too painful to bear. Then, because there was no choice, I said them. "That he was running away from us."

She nodded heavily. "So you have to talk to him, Eric."

"We both do."

"No," Meredith said firmly. "It would look like we were ganging up on him."

"All right," I said. "But I'm going to tell him everything Peak told me. Everything Price told me. And I'm going to ask him who brought him home that night. I want an answer to that."

Meredith released a weary breath.

"I won't take some bullshit story, either," I said. "This is getting worse and worse, and he has to know that."

"Yes," Meredith said. She seemed far away, and getting farther, like a boat unmoored and drifting out into the open sea. "All right," she said. Then she turned and made her way down the corridor to her small office, where I imagined she remained, waiting anxiously for her son to come home.

TWENTY

It was nearly four in the afternoon when Keith appeared.

During the hours before I finally saw Keith peddle down the unpaved driveway, I tried to find the best way to approach him. I remember how clumsy my mother had always been at such interrogations. She would ask Warren about some misdeed. He would deny it. She would accept his denial, and that would be the end of it. My father, on the other hand, had relentlessly pursued him, puncturing each alibi, watching sternly, his eyes gleaming with superiority as my brother steadily sank deeper into the mire of his own inept little falsehoods. If Warren claimed to have been watching television when some small misdeed had been committed, my father would whip out the *TV Guide* and demand to know exactly what Warren had been watching. If Warren were clever enough actually to have named a program, my father would rifle through the pages until he found the show and then demand that Warren tell him precisely what, exactly, the show had been about. He'd always managed to be two or three steps ahead of Warren, waiting for him like a mugger in a dark alleyway, poised to strike.

But Warren had been easy to frighten and confuse. After only a few minutes under my father's inquisition he would invariably surrender, confess what slight crime he'd committed, then accept whatever punishment my father decreed. Warren had always been pliant, straining to please, contrite, eager to say or do whatever my father commanded.

I knew I could not expect the same of Keith. His mood was volatile, resentful, sullen. At the slightest provocation, he might bolt out of the room, storm into the night, make his run for it. More than anything, what I feared as I watched him slip off the seat of his bike and trudge up the walkway toward the house was that in the end it would turn physical, that in order to prevent him from running away, I would have to use force.

He didn't see me when he came through the door. He tossed his book bag on the stairs, whirled to the right, and strode into the kitchen. I heard him open the refrigerator. There was a clink of bottles, the sound of one being opened. I assumed he'd taken a bottled water or a soda, but when he slouched back into the foyer, I saw that he held a beer.

When he saw me sitting in the living room, he stared at me evenly, waiting for a challenge, then tilted back his head, took a long swig, and wiped his mouth with his sleeve.

"You're not of drinking age, Keith," I reminded him.

"That right?" he asked with a smirk. "Well, by the time

I'm old enough to drink, I'll be in jail, so, like they say, what the fuck." He grinned at me defiantly, took another swig, then pressed the bottle toward me. "Care for a drink, Dad?"

I stood up, walked over to him, and yanked the bottle from his hand. "We need to talk," I said. "In your room."

"My room?" He laughed dismissively. "No way, Dad."

I placed the bottle on the table beside the door. "Your room," I said evenly. "Now."

He shook his head with exaggerated weariness, turned, and made his way up the stairs with a slow exhausted gait, like a boy who'd worked in the fields all day, rather than one who'd spent the last seven hours sitting in a classroom.

At the door of his room, he turned to me. "You're not going to like it," he said. "It's not like all neat and orderly."

"I don't care what it looks like," I told him.

With that, Keith opened the door to his room and stepped inside.

I followed behind, stepping into a level of clutter and disarray that I'd fully expected. The only surprise was that between the window and the small desk that had once held his computer, he'd hung a thick black cloth, which was clearly meant to block the monitor from view. The walls of the room were covered with torn-out magazine pictures of people dressed in Goth attire, black jeans and black T-shirts, stringy hair dyed black, blackened eyes and lips and fingernails.

"Like the décor, Dad?" Keith asked with a brutal laugh. "Glad you came to visit?"

I whirled around to face him. "Delmot Price and I had a little talk this morning," I said.

Keith slumped down on the unmade bed and idly picked up a magazine. "So?"

"The police have talked to him, too," I added. "They know you called him the night Amy disappeared."

Keith flipped a page of the magazine, licked his finger, and flipped another. "I just wanted to talk," he said.

"About your plan to run away?"

Keith gave no sign that the fact that I knew about his plan in the least bothered him. He continued to stare at the magazine.

"Look at me, Keith," I said sharply.

He lifted his eyes languidly.

"Put the magazine away."

He flipped the cover, tossed it across the room, and made a great show of staring me directly in the eye.

"First off, don't even think about leaving town," I said. "That's all the cops would need right now."

Keith kicked off his shoes, pressed his back against the wall, and folded his arms over his chest.

I pulled the chair away from his desk, planted it in the center of the room, and sat down so that we were now eye to eye.

"I need some answers, Keith," I said.

Keith said nothing but continued to stare at me sullenly.

"They found pictures on your computer," I said.

I looked for some sign that the shock of having the pictures discovered had shaken him but saw nothing but his cold metallic stare.

"Why did you have those pictures, Keith?"

His silence was like a cocked gun.

"Little girls," I said. "Naked."

He closed his eyes.

"Why did you have pictures of little girls on your computer?"

He shook his head.

"They found them, Keith," I said firmly. "They found them on your computer."

He continued to shake his head, eyes still closed.

"You know what that looks like, don't you? How bad it looks. With Amy missing."

He began to breathe with exaggerated force, rhythmically, like a pant.

"Keith, are you listening to me? They *found pictures*!"

He was breathing in short gasps, loud and furiously, like a diver gearing up for a frightening plunge.

"They showed them to me, Keith," I said. "Little girls. Seven, eight years old."

Suddenly the gasping breaths ceased, and his eyes shot open. "What else?" he hissed. "What else, Dad? I know there's more."

"Yes, there is," I said hotly, as if he'd challenged me to make a stronger case against him. "I want to know who brought you home the night Amy disappeared."

He stared at me silently for a moment, and I expected him to yell back some ridiculous reply, but instead something appeared to unravel deep within him, as if he were suddenly in the motions of a final letting go. "Nobody brought me home."

I leaned forward threateningly. "I saw a car pull into the driveway, Keith. Up on the road. It pulled in. I saw the lights. Then it backed up and drove away. That's when I saw you coming down the drive." I lifted my head and looked him dead in the eye. "Who brought you home in that car, Keith?"

"Nobody," Keith answered softly.

"Keith, I have to know the truth," I said. "I have to know about those pictures. And I have to know about that car."

"I didn't have any pictures," he said with surprising firmness. "And nobody brought me home that night."

I felt nearly drunk with exasperation, dazed and staggering. "Keith, you have to tell me the truth."

Without the slightest warning, a wrenching sob broke from him. It seemed to come from an unexpected depth, a sob that all but gutted him. "Fuck me," he cried. He dropped his head forward then brought it back against the wall so hard that the force rattled the shelf that hung above him. "Fuck me!"

"Jesus, Keith, can't you see I'm trying to help you?"

"Fuck me," Keith cried. He jerked forward, then, like a body caught in a seizure, he slammed his head back against the wall.

I shot out of my chair and jerked the black cloth from the wire. *"No more fucking lies!"* I screamed.

Keith thrust forward, then slammed back again, his head pounding violently against the wall. He seemed caught in an uncontrollable spasm, his body moving like a puppet in the hands of a murderous puppeteer,

I grabbed his shoulders and drew him tightly into my arms. "Stop it, Keith," I pleaded. "Stop it!"

He began to cry again, and I held him while he cried, held him until he finally stopped crying and slumped down on the bed, where he wiped his eyes with the palms of his hands, then looked up and started to speak. That for a moment I thought he'd decided to come clean, admit what there was to admit about the pictures, the car that had brought him home that night. Even at its worst, I thought, it would be a relief to have it out, done with, known. It was the suspense that was killing us, slowly, hour by hour, like a long drawn-out strangulation.

"Keith, please tell me," I said softly.

His lips sealed immediately, and his eyes were dry now. "I didn't do anything," he said softly. He closed his eyes slowly, then opened them again. "I didn't do anything," he repeated. He slithered out of my arms and sat bolt upright on the bed, no longer broken. I felt him harden before my eyes. "May I please be alone now?" he asked stiffly. "I'd really like to be alone."

I knew there was no point in challenging him further. The moment had come and gone. This had been my chance, and his, but nothing had come of it, and it was over.

I walked out of the room and down the stairs to where Meredith now sat in the living room.

"Nothing," I said. "He denied everything."

Her eyes took on a kind of animal panic. "He has to tell you the truth, Eric."

"The truth, yes," I said.

I glanced at the outline of her cell phone in the shallow pocket of her robe and considered all that now demanded to be truly known, things my father had told me, things Warren had told me, things Keith had told me, all of them now in doubt. In my mind I saw them posed together, Meredith and Keith, along with my other family, the living and the dead, Warren and my father, my mother, Jenny. They stood on the steps of the lost house, shoulder to shoulder, as in a family photograph.

None of them was smiling.

PART IV

A figure appears beyond the diner's rain-streaked window, and for a moment you think it is the one you're waiting for. You recall it in photographs, but so much time has passed that you can no longer be sure that you would recognize the eyes, the mouth, the hair. Features sharpen then blur as they mature, and time has a downward pull, creating folds where none existed when the photographs were taken. And so you scan the onrushing faces, preparing your own, hoping that time has not ravaged your features so mercilessly that you will go unrecognized as well.

You notice a little girl, her hand tucked inside her mother's, and it strikes you that everyone was young back then. You were young. So were Meredith and Warren. Keith was young and Amy was young. Vincent and Karen Giordano were young. Peak was no more than fifty; Kraus no more than forty-five. Even Leo Brock seems young to you now, or at least not as old as he seemed then.

The figure who first called your attention vanishes, but you continue to stare out the window. An autumn wind is lashing the trees across the way, showering the wet ground with falling leaves. You think of the Japanese maple at the end of the walkway and recall the last time you saw it. It was fall then, too. You remember your last glance at the house, how your gaze settled on the grill. How desolate it looked beside the empty house, its elaborate and sturdy brickwork awash in sodden leaves. You wonder if you should have taken a picture of the cold grill, the unlit house, something to replace the stacks of family photographs you burned in the fireplace on your last day there. In a movie, a character like you would have fed them one by one into the flames, but you tossed whole stacks of them in at once. You even tried not to look at the faces in the photographs as the fire engulfed them, turning every life to ash.

TWENTY-ONE

Over a week passed after my confrontation with Keith. Day after day, as I worked at the shop, I waited for the call from Leo, the one that would tell me that Keith was going to be arrested, that I should go home, wait for Peak and Kraus to arrive, warrants in hand, and read my son his rights, then, one man at each arm, lead him away.

But when it came, the phone call from Leo brought just the opposite news.

"It's looking good, Eric," he said happily. "They're running tests on those cigarettes they found outside Amy's window, but even if it turns out they can prove Keith smoked them, so what? There's no law against a kid going out for a smoke."

"But he lied, Leo," I said. "He said he didn't leave the house."

225

"Well, contrary to popular belief," Leo said, "lying to the police is not technically a crime. And as for those pictures on his computer? Same answer. They were completely harmless."

Pictures of nude little girls didn't strike me as harmless, but I let it go.

"So, what happens then, if they can't arrest him?" I asked.

"Nothing happens," Leo answered lightly.

"It can't just go away, Leo," I said. "A little girl is missing and—"

"And Keith had nothing to do with it," Leo interrupted. He spoke his next words at a measured pace. "Nothing to do with it, right?"

I didn't answer fast enough, so Leo said, "Right, Eric?"

"Right," I muttered.

"So like I said, it's good news all around," Leo repeated cautiously. "You should take it as good news."

"I know."

"So, is there a reason you're not?"

"It's just that this whole experience, it's dredged up a lot of things," I told him. "Not just about Keith. Other things."

"Things between you and Meredith?"

It seemed an odd question. I'd never discussed the state of my marriage with Leo, yet something "between you and Meredith" was the first thing that had entered his mind. "Why would you think it's something between me and Meredith?" I asked.

"No reason," Leo said. "Except that a case like this, it can create a certain strain." He quickly moved on to another subject. "Everything else okay?"

"Sure."

"No harm to your business, right?"

"Just the usual off-season lull."

There was a pause and I sensed that something bad was coming.

"One thing, Eric," Leo said. "Evidently Vince Giordano's pretty upset."

"Of course, he is," I said. "His daughter is missing."

"Not just that," Leo said. "Upset with the way the case is going."

"You mean, about Keith?"

"That's right," Leo said. "My people tell me he went ballistic at headquarters yesterday. Demanded that Keith be arrested, that sort of thing."

"He thinks Keith did it," I said. "There's nothing I can do about that."

"You can stay clear of him," Leo said in that paternal way of his. "And make sure Keith does, too."

"All right," I said.

"Warren, too."

"Warren?" I asked, surprised. "Why would he have anything against Warren?"

"Because Keith doesn't have a car," Leo told me. "So Vince figures it had to be the two of them."

"Why would he think that?"

"We're not dealing with reason here, Eric," Leo reminded me. "We're talking about a distraught father. So just tell everyone in your family to stay clear of Vince. And if any of you happen to run into him, like at the post office, something like that, just keep to yourself, and get out of sight as soon as possible."

There was a brief pause, then Leo spoke again, his voice now unexpectedly gentle. "Are you all right, Eric?"

A wave of deep melancholy washed over me; my life, my once-comfortable life, was fraught with danger and confusion, along with a terrible mixture of anger and pain. "How could I be all right, Leo?" I asked. "Everyone in town thinks Keith killed Amy Giordano. Some anonymous caller tells the cops that there's 'something wrong' with me or Meredith or Keith. And now I hear Vince has gone nuts and that none of us can go anywhere without fear of running into him. It's a prison, Leo. That's where we all are right now. We're in prison."

Again there was a pause, after which, Leo said, "Eric, I want you to listen very carefully to me. In all likelihood, Keith is not going to be arrested. That's good news, and you should be happy about it. And if some nut calls the hotline? Big deal. And as far as Vince Giordano is concerned, all you have to do is stay away from him."

"Okay," I muttered. What was the point of saying more?

"Do you understand what I'm telling you?"

"Yeah," I said. "Thanks for calling Leo."

Leo was clearly reluctant to hang up. "Good news, remember?" he said, addressing a schoolboy in need of a change of attitude.

"Good news, yes," I said, though only because I knew it was what he wanted to hear. "Good news," I repeated, then smiled as if for a hidden camera in my shop, planted by Leo, so that even at that moment he could see my face, appreciate the smile.

My working day came to an end a few hours later, but I didn't want to go home. Meredith had told me that she'd be working late at the college, and I knew that Keith would be secreted in his room. And so I called Warren, hoping he could join me for a beer, but there was no answer.

That left only my father, and so I went to him.

He was sitting inside, by the fire, curled in a wheelchair, his emaciated frame wrapped in a dark red blanket. In his youth, he'd gone all winter without once putting on an overcoat, but now even a slight late-September touch of fall chilled him.

"It's not Thursday," he said as I came up the stairs.

I sat down in the wicker chair beside him. "I just felt like dropping in," I told him.

He stared into the flames. "Warren talk to you?"

"Yeah."

"That why you're here?"

I shook my head.

"I figured he'd go whining to you, try to get me to change my mind, let him come over again."

"No, he didn't do that," I said. "He told me you had an argument, that you said you didn't want to see him again, but he wasn't whining about it."

My father's eyes narrowed hatefully. "Should have done it long ago," he said coldly. "Worthless."

"Worthless," I repeated. "That's what you said about Mom."

He peered about absently, like a man in a museum full of artifacts he had no interest in.

"Speaking of which," I said. "You lied to me, Dad."

He closed his eyes wearily, clearly preparing himself for yet another series of false accusations.

"You said you didn't take out an insurance policy on Mom," I continued. "I found it in your papers. It was for two hundred thousand dollars." When this had no visible effect on my father, I added, "Why did you lie to me about this, Dad?"

His gaze slid over to me. "I didn't."

A wave of anger swept over me, fueled by exasperation. My father was doing the same thing Keith had done a week before.

"Dad, I found an application for a life insurance policy," I snapped.

"An application is not a policy, Eric," my father scoffed. "You should know that."

"Are you denying there was ever such a policy?" I demanded. "Is that what you're doing?"

A dry laugh broke from him. "Eric, you asked me if I took out a policy on your mother. I said I didn't. Which is the truth."

"Once again, Dad, are you saying there was no life insurance policy on Mom's life?"

"As a matter of fact, Eric, I'm not saying that at all."

"So there was one?"

"Yes."

"For two hundred thousand dollars?"

"That was the amount," my father said. "But does that mean I took the policy out?"

"Who else would?"

"Your mother, Eric," my father said flatly. "Your mother took it out."

"On herself?"

"Yes." His eyes glistened slightly, though I couldn't be sure if the glistening came from some well of lost emotion, or if it were only an illusion, merely a play of light. "She took it out without telling me," he added. "She had a . . . friend. He helped her do it."

"A friend?"

"Yes," my father answered. "You met him. A family friend." His smile was more a sneer. "Good friend of your mother. Always coming around the house. Glad to be of help, that was Jason."

"Jason," I said. "Benefield?"

"So, you've heard about him?"

"Warren mentioned him," I explained.

"Of course," my father said with an odd, downward jerk at the corners of his mouth. "Anyway, he's still alive. You can ask him. He'll tell you I had nothing to do with that policy. And for your added information, I wasn't the beneficiary of it, either."

I couldn't tell if this was a bluff, but I suspected that it was, and moved to expose it. "Where did the money go?" I asked.

"What money?"

"The money that was due after Mom died."

"There was never any money, Eric," my father said. "Not a penny."

"Why not?"

He hesitated, and in that interval, I imagined all the worthless get-rich-quick schemes into which he had probably poured the money, a bottomless pit of failed businesses and bad investments.

"The company denied the claim," he said finally.

He squirmed uncomfortably, and I knew he was trying to get off the hook. So I bore in.

"Why did the company deny the claim?" I asked.

"Ask them yourself," my father shot back.

"I'm asking you," I said hotly.

My father turned away from me.

"Tell me, goddamn it!"

His eyes shot over to me. "Insurance companies don't pay," he said, "when it's a suicide."

"Suicide?" I whispered unbelievingly. "You're telling me that Mom intended to run off that bridge? That's ridiculous."

My father's glare was pure challenge. "Then why wasn't she wearing a seat belt, Eric? She always insisted on wearing one, remember? She made all of you wear them. So why, on that particular day, when she went off that bridge, did she not have hers on?"

He read the look in my eyes.

"You don't believe me, do you?" he asked.

"No, I don't."

"Then look at the police report. It was all right there— the whole story: How fast she was going. The way the car went straight into the guardrail—everything. Including the fact that she wasn't wearing a seat belt." He shook his head. "There were witnesses, too. People who saw what she did." A contemptuous laugh broke from him. "Couldn't even pull off a simple suicide scheme without fucking it up."

"Don't lie to me, Dad," I warned. "Not about this."

"Go look at the fucking report, if you don't believe me," my father snarled. "There's a copy in my files. You've been digging around in them anyway, right? Dig some more."

I couldn't let him go unchallenged. "Speaking of your files," I said. "I found a letter from Aunt Emma. She blames Mom for spending you into bankruptcy."

My father waved his hand. "Who cares what my nutty sister writes?"

"It's what you wrote that bothered me."

"Which was?"

"A line you scrawled in the margin of Aunt Emma's letter."

"I repeat, 'Which was?'"

"'Now let her get me out of it.'"

My father laughed. "Jesus, Eric."

"What did you mean by that?"

"That Emma should get me out of it," my father said. "She's the 'her' in that note."

"How could Aunt Emma get you out of it?"

"Because her goddamn husband left her a fortune," my father said. "But true to form, she never spent a dime of it. And she wouldn't have given me a penny, either. When she died, she still had every dollar that old bastard left her. Close to a million dollars. You know where it went? To a fucking animal shelter!"

He laughed again, but bitterly, as if all he had ever known of life amounted to little more than a cruel joke.

I waited until his laughter faded, then, because I couldn't stop myself, I asked the final question. "Did Mom have an affair? Warren said she did. With that man you mentioned, Benefield. He said Aunt Emma told you about it."

For a moment, my father seemed unable to deal with this latest assault. "What is this all about, Eric? All this business about insurance policies, affairs. What have you been thinking?" He saw the answer in my eyes. "You thought I killed her, didn't you? Either for money or because I thought she was fucking around. One or the other, right?" He released a scoffing chuckle. "Does it matter which one it is, Eric?" He didn't wait for me to answer. "This is all about Keith, isn't it?" he asked. "You can't bear to think that he may be a liar and a murderer, so you've decided to think it about me." He remained silent for a few seconds. I could see his mind working behind his darting eyes, reasoning something through, coming to a grave conclusion. Then he looked at me. "Well, if you're so fucking eager to find the truth about this, Eric, here's a truth you might wish you hadn't heard." His grin was pure triumph. "I wasn't the beneficiary of your mother's insurance policy. You were."

I stared at him, thunderstruck. "Me? Why would she . . . ?"

"She knew how much you wanted to go to college," my father interrupted. He shrugged with a curious sense of acceptance. "It was the only way she could make sure you had the money you needed."

I didn't believe him, and yet at the same time what he said made sense. In the grips of that dire uncertainty, I realized that there was absolutely nothing I could be sure of. I saw the car's yellow beams sweep through the undergrowth and thought of Keith's lie. And here was my father telling me that my mother had driven the family station wagon off a thirty-foot bridge, a story that could just as easily be used to shift my own suspicions concerning my mother's death safely away from him.

I got to my feet. "I'm leaving," I told him.

This time, my father made no effort to stop me. "Suit yourself," he said.

"I'm not sure I'll be coming back, Dad," I added sourly.

He stared at the fire. "Have I ever asked you to come here?" His eyes slithered over to me. "Have I ever asked you for one fucking thing, Eric?" Before I could answer he whipped his eyes away and settled them angrily on the lashing flames. "Just go."

I hesitated a moment longer, let my gaze take him in, the bony shoulders beneath the robe, the shrunken eyes, how at this moment he had absolutely nothing, a penury deeper than I'd have imagined possible only a few days before. But I could not approach him now, felt not the slightest inclination to re-gain any footing for us. And with that recognition, I knew that this was the last time I would see my father alive.

I took in the scene with a quick blink of the eye, then wheeled around and returned to my car. Slumped behind the wheel, I hesitated, glancing back toward the bleak little resi-dence where I knew my father was doomed to slog through what remained of his days. He would grow brittle and still more bitter, I supposed, speaking sharply to anyone who approached him. In time, both staff and fellow residents would learn to keep their distance, so that in the final hour, when they came and found him slumped in his chair or faceup in bed, a little wave of secret pleasure would sweep through the halls and common rooms at the news of his death. Such would be his parting gift to his fellow man—the brief relief of knowing that he was gone.

TWENTY-TWO

As I drove toward home, mother's long ordeal returned to me in a series of small grainy photographs that seemed to rise from some previously forgotten album in my mind. I saw her standing beneath the large oak that graced our neatly manicured front lawn. I saw her walking in the rain. I saw her lying awake in a dark bedroom, her face illuminated by a single white candle. I saw her in the dimly lit garage, sitting alone behind the wheel of the dark blue Chrysler, her hands in her lap, head slightly bowed.

In fact, I had only glimpsed these images of my mother's final weeks, glimpsed them as I'd hurried past her on my way to school or returned from it, far more interested in the day's boyish transactions than in the adult world that was eating her alive.

But now, as evening fell, I tried to measure the weight that lay upon her: an unloving and unsuccessful husband, a beloved daughter dead, a son—Warren—saddled with his father's contempt, and me, the other son, who barely saw her when he passed. So little to leave behind, she must have thought, as she sat behind the wheel in the shadowy garage, so little she would miss.

For the first time in years, I felt burdened beyond my strength, desperate to share the load with another human being. It was at that moment, I suppose, that the full value of marriage proclaimed itself. I had laughed at a thousand jokes about married life. And what a huge target it was, after all. The idea that you would share your entire life with one person, expect that man or woman to satisfy a vast array of needs, from the most passionate to the most mundane—on its face, it was absurd. How could it ever work?

Suddenly, I knew. It worked because in a shifting world you wanted one person you could trust to be there when you needed her.

It was a short ride down Route 6, no more than twenty minutes. The college sat on a rise, all brick and glass, one of those purely functional structures architects despise, but whose charmlessness is hardly noticed by the legions of students who obliviously come and go. It was a junior college, after all, a holding cell between high school and university, unremarkable and doomed to be unremembered, save as a launching pad toward some less-humble institution.

I pulled into the lot designated VISITORS, and made my way up the cement walkway toward Meredith's office. In the distance, I could see her car parked in the lot reserved for faculty, and something in its sturdy familiarity was oddly comforting.

Meredith's office was on the second floor. I knocked, but there was no answer. I glanced at the office hours she'd posted on the door, 4:30 to 6:30. I glanced at my watch. It was 5:45, so I assumed Meredith would be back soon, that she'd gone to the bathroom or was lingering in the faculty lounge.

A few folding metal chairs dotted the corridor, places where students could seat themselves while waiting for their scheduled appointments. I sat down, plucked a newspaper from the chair next to me, and idly went through it. There was little about Amy's disappearance, save that the police were still "following various leads."

I perused the paper a few more minutes, then glanced at my watch. It was 6:05. I looked down the empty corridor, hoping to see Meredith at the end of it. I even imagined her coming through the double doors, munching an apple, the early-evening snack she often took in order to quell her appetite before coming home.

But the corridor remained empty, and so I went through the paper again, this time reading articles that didn't interest me very much, the sports and financial pages, something about a new treatment for baldness.

When I'd read the last of them, I put down the paper and again looked at my watch. 6:15.

I stood up, walked to her office, and knocked again on the unlikely chance that she hadn't heard me the first time. There was no answer, but I could see a sliver of light coming from inside. She'd left the lights on, something she wouldn't have done if she hadn't been planning to come back.

On that evidence, I returned to my chair and waited. As the minutes passed, I thought again of my father, the terrible things he'd told me, which I suddenly believed were true. I don't know why I came to that conclusion as I sat waiting for Meredith that evening, only that with each passing second, the certainty built, and one by one, every dark suspicion took on a fatal substance. I believed that my mother had had an affair. I believed that she'd taken out an insurance policy on herself. I believed that she'd committed suicide. But at the same time, I also believed that my father had wanted her dead, might even have toyed with the idea of killing her, perhaps even killing us all.

I felt the air darken around me, thicken like smoke, felt my breathing take on a strange, frantic pace, as if I were being forced to run faster and faster along an unlit path, to leap obstacles I could barely see and twist around gaping pits and snares. A kind of rumbling shook me from within, distant as a building storm, and I found myself staring at the sliver of light beneath Meredith's door wondering if perhaps she were actually inside, knew I was in the corridor, but remained behind the locked door . . . hiding.

But from what?

I stood suddenly, jerked up by my own volcanic anxiety, marched to the door, and knocked again, this time harder, more insistently. Then, out of nowhere, her name broke from my lips in a strange, animal cry—*"Meredith!"*

I realized that I'd called her name much more loudly than

I'd intended. I could hear it echoing down the hall. It sounded desperate, even theatrical, like Stanley Kowalski screaming for Stella.

I took a deep breath and tried to calm myself, but my skin felt hot, and beneath it, hotter still, as if deep inside, a furnace was being madly stoked.

It was past 6:30 now, and as I looked at the otherwise inconsequential time of day, it took on a fatal quality, like the hour of execution, the prisoner now being led out. It was as if I had given my wife until that moment to explain herself, which she had failed to do, and so was now condemned.

I strode down the corridor, taking the stairs two at a time, and plunged through the doors out into the crisp, cold air. For a moment, the chill cooled my burning skin, but only briefly, because in the distance, at the end of the lot, in the space between her car and a sleek BMW, I saw Meredith standing with a tall slender man.

Rodenberry.

I darted behind a nearby tree and watched them with the skulking silence of a Peeping Tom. They stood very close to each other, talking intimately. From time to time Rodenberry nodded, and from time to time, Meredith reached out and touched his arm.

I waited for them to draw together into each other's arms, waited like a man in a darkened theater, waited for the kiss that would seal both their fates.

It didn't matter that it never came. It didn't matter that after a final word, Meredith simply turned and walked to her car, and that Rodenberry, with the same casualness, got into the gleaming BMW. It only mattered that as each of them drove away, I heard the click of the police hotline, then the whisper that came through the line, and knew absolutely who had spoken and what had been said.

When, in the throes of crisis, you have nowhere to go but to a lawyer, you should realize just how depleted you have become. But I was far from realizing anything that night, and so I went to Leo Brock.

His office was modest, simply a small brick building tucked between a gourmet deli and a hardware store. His far more impressive Mercedes was parked in a space reserved for it behind the office.

His secretary had already gone home for the evening, but the door to his office was open, and I found Leo in the leather chair behind his desk, feet up, idly thumbing a magazine.

"Eric," he said with a big smile. "How's it going?"

He must have known that it could not have been going very well if I were here, standing before his desk, looking shaken, like a man who'd stared into the pit and seen the dreadful face of things.

"You had another run in with Vincent?" he asked immediately.

"No."

He drew his feet from the top of the desk, and in that gesture I read just how dire I appeared to him. "What is it, Eric?" he asked.

"That thing on the hotline," I said. "What was it?"

He unnecessarily slid the magazine to the corner of his desk. "It was nothing," he said.

"What do you mean nothing?"

"Eric, why don't you sit down."

"What do you mean, nothing, Leo?"

"I mean it had nothing to do with the case."

"Keith's case."

"The Amy Giordano case," Leo corrected.

"But you know what it was?"

"I have an idea."

"What was it?"

"As I said, Eric, it had nothing to do with the case."

"And as I said, Leo, what the fuck was it?"

He looked at me as if sparks were flying off my body, gathering in glowing clusters on his oriental carpet.

"Eric, please, have a seat."

I recalled how he and Meredith had stood together in the driveway of the house, speaking in what now seemed secretive tones, how Leo had nodded to her reassuringly, how my wife's hands had then dropped limply to her sides as if she'd just shuffled off a heavy weight.

"I knew from the beginning," I said.

"Knew what?"

"Knew that Meredith told you."

Leo looked at me with what was clearly a fake expression of bafflement.

"That first day," I said, "when you came over to talk with Keith. Meredith walked you to your car. That's when she told you."

"Told me what?"

"Told you that there were things in the family," I said. "Things that were . . . wrong. I even know why she did it. She was afraid that in the end it would come out anyway. What she didn't know is that other people knew. At least one person."

Leo leaned back in his chair and opened his arms. "Eric, I don't have a clue what you're talking about."

"At the car, the two of you," I explained.

"Yes, she walked me out to my car, so what?"

"That's when she told you."

Leo looked both worried and exasperated, like a man before a cobra, wary, but also growing tired of its dance. "You're going to have to be a tad more specific as to exactly what it is you think she said to me on that occasion."

I recalled Meredith's voice as I'd come home that afternoon, taking her by surprise, the quick way she'd blurted, "Gotta go," then sunk the phone into her pocket. A series of memories followed that initial recollection: Meredith working late at the college; the wistful tone in which she'd said, "It will be the last time"; how it hadn't been Dr. Mays who'd told her the Lenny Bruce story; the fact that Mays had described Stuart Rodenberry as "very funny." Last, I saw Meredith once again in the parking lot with Rodenberry, pressed closely together, as I saw it, but duly cautious not to touch.

"That she was having an affair," I said quietly, like a man finally accepting a terrible, terrible truth. "That's what the police heard on the hotline. That Meredith is having an affair."

Leo stared at me mutely, a pose I had no doubt was part of a deception. He was almost as much in league with Meredith as Rodenberry, all three of them arrayed against me, determined to keep me in the dark,

"Here's another guess," I said sharply. "The person who called the hotline was a woman, wasn't it?"

Leo leaned forward and peered at me closely. "Eric, you need to calm down."

I rebuked him with a harsh cackle. "The wife of the man Meredith is supposed to be having an affair with, that's who called."

Leo now looked as if deep in thought, unable to decide between two equally difficult choices.

"A pale little wisp of a thing named Judith Rodenberry," I added.

Leo shook his head. "I don't know what you're talking about, Eric," he said.

He was lying, and I knew it. Again, I recalled that first day, when Meredith had walked him to his black Mercedes, the two of them standing there in the driveway, half concealed by the spreading limbs of the Japanese maple, but not concealed so much that I hadn't seen the way Meredith's hands fluttered about like panicked birds until a few no-doubt well-chosen words from Leo stopped them in their frenzied flight. What had he said?, I wondered now, then instantly put the words into his mouth: *Don't worry, Meredith, no one will find out.*

"Did you hear me, Eric?" Leo said firmly. "I have no idea what you're talking about. The hotline matter, it had nothing to do with Meredith."

"What then?" I challenged. "What did this person say? What was this 'something wrong'?" I felt like a vial filled to the brim with combustible materials, everything poised at the volcanic edge. *"Tell me the fucking truth!"*

Leo slumped back in his chair and seemed almost to grow older before my eyes, more grave in his demeanor than I had ever seen him. "Warren," he said. "The 'something wrong' is Warren."

TWENTY-THREE

In all the years I'd gone there, the scores and scores of times, I'd never noticed anything. But now as I turned onto Warren's street, I noticed everything. I noticed how close his house was to the elementary school, how his upstairs window looked out over the school's playground, how, from that small, square window, he could easily watch the girls on the swings, see their skirts lift and fold back as they glided forward. He could stand behind the translucent white curtains and observe them clamoring over the monkey bars and riding up and down on the seesaw. Or, if he wished, he could stare down at the entire playground, take in small gatherings of little girls at a single glimpse, keep track of them as they played, pick and choose among them, find the one that most interested him and follow her like a hunter tracking a deer caught in the crosshairs of his scope.

As I closed in upon his house, I thought of other things, too. I recalled that Warren preferred to work on weekends and take Wednesdays and Thursdays off, both school days, days when the little girls of the elementary school would be frolicking on the playground. I remembered how he never minded working holidays, when school was out, and how each year, he seemed to dread the approach of summer, when school would no longer be in session. He had reasons for all these preferences, of course. He didn't mind working weekends, he said, because he didn't have anything to do anyway. He didn't mind working holidays because holidays depressed him, which, in turn made it harder for him to resist the bottle. He dreaded summer because it was hot and muggy, and he didn't like to work in heat and humidity.

In the past, his reasons had always made perfect sense to me. Now they seemed fabrications, ways of concealing the fact that what my brother wanted to do more than anything was to stand at his window and peer down at the elementary school playground and watch little girls at play.

These thoughts led me to a yet darker one, hurling my mind back to the month when Warren had been holed up at my house with a broken hip. Holed up in Keith's room. With Keith's computer. I could almost hear the tap of his fingers on the keys as I had so many times when I'd walked by the closed door of Keith's room when Warren was staying there. At the time, I'd assumed that Warren was playing some mindless computer game.

Then I thought of the pictures Detective Peak had shown me, pictures taken from Keith's computer, and remembered the anguish of Keith's denial, the way he'd banged his head against the wall, how fiercely he had fought off the horror of my accusations. Now I knew that it had been Warren all along, Warren who'd sat hour after hour cruising the Internet for pictures of little girls. The only question now was what he saw in them. What in the twisted circuitry of my brother's mind allowed him to drag these little girls from the safety of their childhoods and harness their small undeveloped bodies to his adult desire?

I tried to recall if I'd ever seen the slightest sign of such a dark perversity. I went back through the days and years of our youth, the times we'd been together in the presence of small children, and searched for some glimmer in Warren's eye, a look I might not have understood at that earlier time, but which I would easily recognize now. Had his gaze ever followed a child across a yard or down a street? Had he ever stopped in midsentence at a little girl's approach? Had he ever so much as mentioned a neighborhood kid, someone's little sister, perhaps, or a visiting cousin?

I could find no instance of any such early indication, not one occasion when Warren had seemed anything but an awkward boy, lacking in self-confidence, slow in his studies, incompetent on the playing field, the butt of countless school-yard jokes. He'd been all these things, and in one way or another I'd always felt sorry for him. But now I felt nothing but revulsion, a creepy sense that this boy had grown into an utterly repulsive man.

I pulled into Warren's driveway behind the battered truck he used in his work. Its open bed was scattered with paint cans and spattered drop cloths, and two equally spattered wooden ladders were strapped to its sideboards, loosely tied and drooping, as I would have expected from Warren. All his life he'd done things haphazardly, with little attention to detail, following a course as wobbly as his footsteps when he'd had too much to drink. Even so, I'd always had a brother's affection for him, overlooked his lassitude, his drinking, those parts of his life that were basically pathetic. But now a vile shadow covered him, my suspicions so intense, and in their intensity, so brutal, that I couldn't ignore them.

And yet, for all that, I sat behind the wheel for a long time, sat in Warren's weedy driveway, unable to move, staring at the small bleak house he'd lived in for fifteen years. His door was closed, of course, but a sickly yellow light shone from the upstairs room he called his bachelor lair. He'd furnished the room with a motley assortment of furniture, along with a television, a computer, and a refrigerator just large enough to hold a few six packs of beer. He'd lit the place with lava lamps at one point, then a series of garish paper lanterns, but these had ultimately given way to the single uncovered ceiling light and the flickering of his computer screen.

The image of Warren's dissolute body slumped in an overstuffed chair, his doughy face eerily lit by the computer screen sent a piercing melancholy through me. I saw the weary run of my brother's life, the corrosive nature of his most guarded secret, the unspeakable cravings that ceaselessly gnawed at him. One by one the photographs Detective Peak had found on Keith's computer surfaced in my mind, little girls in nature, naked, innocent, incapable of arousing anything but a child-man. But that was what Warren was, wasn't he? Stunted in every way a man can be stunted, dismal in his own sickly underdevelopment, a wretched, pitiable creature, hardly a man at all.

But none of that, I decided, changed what he had done. He had come into my house, lived in my son's room, and while living there, had poisoned Keith's computer with pictures of naked little girls. And when Keith's computer was seized by the police, he'd kept the fact secret that such incriminating material might still be floating about in its unknowable circuitry. He had sat back silently, knowing full well that the pictures the police found would be laid at Keith's door.

Suddenly, whatever pity I'd felt for Warren vanished, replaced by a stinging anger that he had been perfectly willing to feed my son, his own nephew, to the dogs.

When he answered the door, he was clearly surprised to see me. His eyes were watery and red-rimmed, his cheeks flushed. There was an odd grogginess and imbalance in his posture, so that he seemed almost to teeter as he stood before me in the doorway.

"Hey, Bro," he said softly. He lifted his hand, his finger tightening around a can of beer. "Want a drink?"

"No, thanks."

"What's up?"

"I need to talk to you, Warren."

A gray veil fell over his eyes. "The last time you had to talk to me, I didn't like it very much."

"It's more serious this time," I said grimly. "Something the police found out. Something about you."

I wanted the look in his eyes to be genuine surprise, because if I saw surprise, then I knew I would force myself to entertain the hope that it could all be explained, every detail of what Leo had told me as I stood, dumbstruck in his office. I wanted Warren to explain away the fact that school officials had reported him for staring out his window at the playground, to explain the pictures on Keith's computer, all of it miraculously a mistake. But I didn't see surprise. I saw resignation, a little boy who'd been caught at something disreputable. There was a hint of embarrassment, too, so that I thought he might actually come out with it without my asking, simply tell me to my face that he knew what I was talking about, and that, yes, it was true.

But instead of an admission, he simply shrugged, stepped back into the foyer of his house and said, "Okay, come in."

I followed him into the living room, where he switched on a standing lamp, plopped down on a cracked Naugahyde sofa, and took a quick sip of beer. "Sure you don't want one?" he asked.

"I'm sure."

He sucked in a long breath. "Okay, shoot," he said. "What's on your mind, Bro?"

I sat down in the wooden rocker a few feet away, a relic from the grand house, probably an antique, but worthless now because Warren had taken no care to protect it from scrapes and cuts. "They found pictures on Keith's computer," I began.

Warren lowered his gaze, all the proof I needed that he'd done exactly what I suspected.

"They were of little girls," I added. "Naked little girls."

Warren took a long pull on the beer, but held his gaze on the floor.

"Keith says he never downloaded any pictures like that," I added. "He absolutely denies that they're his."

Warren nodded heavily. "Okay."

"The police checked on when the pictures were downloaded," I said though I had no real proof of this. To this bluff, I added another. "You can do that, you know. You can find out." I watched Warren for any sign that he might come clean. "The exact dates. Literally, to the minute."

Warren shifted uneasily in his chair, but otherwise gave no hint that he could see where I was going with all this, how relentlessly I was closing in.

"They were all downloaded a year ago, Warren," I said. I could not be sure of this, but in my dark world, a lie designed to expose other, darker lies seemed like a ray of light. "Last September." I looked at him pointedly. "You remember where you were last September?"

Warren nodded.

"You were staying in Keith's room," I told him. "You were using Keith's computer. No one else was using it."

Warren lowered the beer to his lap, cradling it between his large flabby thighs. "Yeah," he said softly.

I leaned back in the chair and waited.

"Yeah, okay," Warren said.

Again, I waited, but Warren simply took another sip of beer, then glanced over at me silently.

"Warren," I said pointedly. "Those pictures are yours."

One fat leg began to rock tensely.

"Little girls," I said. "Naked little girls."

The steady rock grew more intense and agitated.

"And then I learned that some people at the school have complained about you," I said. "In the past, I mean. Complained about you watching the kids. Somebody reported that on the police hotline."

"I just look out my window, that's all," he said. The leg rocked violently for a few more seconds then stopped abruptly. "I wouldn't hurt a little girl." He looked lost, but more than that, inwardly disheveled, a crumpled soul, but for all I knew this was no more than a ruse.

"Then why do you watch them, Warren?" I demanded. "And why did you download those pictures?"

Warren shrugged. "They were pretty, the pictures."

A wave of exasperation swept over me. "They were little girls, for Christ's sake!" I cried. "Eight years old. And they were naked!"

"They didn't have to be naked," Warren said weakly, his voice little more than a whine.

"What are you talking about?" I barked. "They were naked, Warren."

"But they didn't have to be, that's what I'm saying." He looked at me like a small child desperately trying to explain himself. "I mean, I don't . . . need them to be naked."

"Need?" I glared at him. "What exactly do you need, Warren?"

"I just like to . . . look at them," he whimpered.

"Little girls?" I fired at him. "You need to look at little

girls?" I bolted forward, my eyes like lasers. "Warren, did you know those pictures were on Keith's computer?"

He shook his head violently. "I didn't. I swear I didn't. I tried to—"

"Erase them, yes, I know." I interrupted. "The cops know it, too."

"I can't help it, Eric."

"Can't help what?"

"You know, looking . . . at . . ." He shook his head. "It's sick. I know it's sick, but I can't help it." He began to cry. "They're just so . . . adorable."

Adorable.

The word leaped in me like a flame. "Adorable," I repeated, all but shaking with the vision my mind instantly created, Warren coming out of Jenny's room that final morning, his face wreathed in what I had taken for exhaustion, but now saw as a scalding shame. "You always said that about"—I saw my sister as she lay in her bed later that same afternoon, her eyes darting about frantically. She'd seemed desperate to tell me something, her lips fluttering in my ear, until suddenly they'd stopped and I'd glanced back toward the door and seen Warren standing there, head bowed, his hands deep in his pockets— "about Jenny."

He saw it in my eyes, the searing accusation that had suddenly seized me.

"Eric," he whispered. He seemed to come out of his stupor, all the day's accumulated drink abruptly draining from him. It was as if he'd been dipped in icy water, then jerked out of it to face a reality colder still. "You think . . . ?"

I wanted to howl *no! no!*, deny in the most passionate and conclusive terms that I had the slightest suspicion that he had ever harmed Jenny, that even his most desperate urge would have stopped at her bed, her helplessness, that as she lay dying, pale and wracked with suffering, he could not possibly have found her . . . adorable.

But the words wouldn't come, and so I only faced him silently.

He stared at me a moment in frozen disbelief. Then he shook his head wearily and pointed to the door. "I'm done with you, Eric," he said. His wet eyes went dry as a desert waste. "I'm done with everything." He pointed to the door. "Go," he said, "just go."

I knew nothing else to do. And so I rose, walked silently out of the room and back to my car. As I pulled out, I saw the light flash upstairs in Warren's bachelor lair and imagined him there alone, sunk in this new despair, wifeless, childless, motherless, fatherless, and now without a brother, too.

I drove back home in a kind of daze, Meredith, Warren, Keith—all of them swirling around in my head like bits of paper in foaming water. I tried to position myself somehow, get a grip on what I knew and didn't know, the dreadful suspicions I could neither avoid nor address, since they were made of smoke and fog.

I pulled in the driveway a few minutes later, got out of the car, swept past the branches of the Japanese maple and headed on down the walkway to the front door.

Through the window, I saw Meredith clutching the phone. She seemed very nearly frantic, her eyes wide in an unmistakable look of alarm. I thought of the other time I'd come upon her abruptly, the way she'd blurted, "Talk to you later," and quickly snapped her cell phone shut and sunk it deep into the pocket of her robe. I had caught her again, I supposed, and, with that thought, fully expected her to hang up immediately when she heard me open the door.

But when I opened the door, she rushed over to me, the phone trembling in her hand. "It's—Warren," she said. "He's drunk and"—she thrust the phone toward me almost violently—"Here," she blurted. "He's yours."

I took the phone. "Warren?"

There was no answer, but I could hear him breathing rapidly, like someone who'd just completed a long exhausting run.

"Warren?" I said again.

Silence.

"Warren," I snapped. "Either talk to me or get the fuck off the phone."

The silence continued briefly, then I heard him draw in a long slow breath.

"Bro," he said softly, "your troubles are over."

Then I heard the blast.

TWENTY-FOUR

The ambulance and police had already arrived by the time I got to Warren's house. The whole neighborhood strobed with flashing lights, and a yellow tape had been stretched across the driveway and along the borders of the yard.

I had called 911 immediately, though even at that moment, I wasn't sure exactly what Warren had done. He'd been drunk, after all, and on such occasions in the past, he'd not been above making some melodramatic gesture in order to win me back. Once, as a boy, he'd taken a plunge off a high embankment after I'd yelled at him. He'd pulled similar stunts after my father had laced into him for one reason or another. It was a pitiful attempt to regain whatever he thought he'd lost in our affection, and it had never worked. Warren had never been one to learn from experience, however, and even as I watched the flashing lights that surrounded his house, I half expected to see him stagger out into the yard, arms spread in greeting, all bleary good cheer. *Hey, Bro.*

But as I closed in on the house, I knew that this time, it was different. The front door was wide open, and Peak stood, backlit by the light of the foyer, scribbling in a small notebook.

"Is he okay?" I asked as I came up to him.

Peak sank the notebook into his jacket pocket. "He's dead," he told me. "I'm sorry."

I didn't shudder at the news, and even now I can hardly recall exactly what I felt, save the curious realization that I would never see my brother alive again. A moment ago, he'd spoken to me. Now he was utterly and forever silent. If I thought or felt more than this at that moment, then those feelings were too vague and insubstantial to make a sustained impression.

"Do you want to identify him?" Peak asked.

"Yes."

"Mind if I ask you a few questions first?"

I shook my head. "I've gotten used to questions."

He drew the notebook out of his pocket and flipped it open. "You spoke to him just before he did it, right?"

"I heard the shot."

This did not faze Peak, and for a moment it struck me that he probably thought it a way of gaining the sympathy he was not inclined to offer.

"What did he say?"

"That my troubles were over," I answered.

"What did he mean by that?"

"That he wouldn't be a bother to me anymore, I guess."

Peak looked at me doubtfully. "You don't think this had anything to do with Amy Giordano?"

"Just the pictures you found on Keith's computer," I said. "They were his."

"How do you know?"

"Warren stayed at our house while he was recovering from a broken hip," I said. "He stayed in Keith's room."

"That doesn't mean the pictures were his," Peak said.

"I know they weren't Keith's."

"How do you know?"

I shrugged. "Why would Warren have done this if the pictures weren't his?"

"Well, he might have thought we'd shift away from Keith," Peak said. "I mean, he all but confessed, didn't he?"

"No, he didn't," I said. "Except that the pictures were his. But he said they weren't . . . sexual. That he didn't use them that way."

"Then why did he have them?"

"He said he just thought the kids were . . . adorable."

Peak looked at me squarely. "Do you think he had anything to do with Amy Giordano being missing?"

I gave the only answer I could be certain of. "I don't know."

Peak looked surprised by my answer. "He was your brother. If he were capable of something like that, kidnapping a little girl, you'd know it, wouldn't you?"

I thought of all the years I'd spent with Warren and realized that for all we'd shared, parents, the big house we'd lost together, the joint trajectories of our lives, for all that, I simply couldn't answer Peak's question, couldn't in the least be sure that I knew Warren at all, or knew any more than his glossy surfaces. "Can you ever know anyone?" I asked.

Peak released a long frustrated breath and closed the notebook. "All right." He glanced inside the house, then back at me. "You ready to make the identification?"

"Yes."

Peak turned and led me up the stairs, then down the short corridor to Warren's room. At the door, he stepped aside. "Sorry," he murmured. "This is never easy."

Warren had pulled a chair up to the window, facing out toward the elementary school's dimly lit playground. His head was slumped to the right, so that he looked as if he'd simply gone to sleep while staring out the window. It was only when I stepped around to face the chair that I saw the shattered mouth, the dead eyes.

I don't know what I felt as I stared down at him during the next few seconds. Perhaps I was simply numb, my tumorous suspicion now grown so large that it was pressing against other vital channels, blocking light and air,

"Was that all he said?" Peak asked. "Just that your troubles were over?"

I nodded.

"How about before he spoke to you? Did he talk to anyone else in your family?"

"You mean Keith, right?" I asked.

"I mean anybody."

"Well, he didn't talk to Keith. He talked to my wife briefly, but not to Keith."

"What did he say to your wife?"

"I don't know," I told him. "When I got home, she handed me the phone. Then Warren said that my troubles were over—nothing else. When I heard the shot, I called 911, then came directly here."

"You came alone, I noticed."

"Yes."

Peak looked as if he felt sorry for me because I'd had to come to the scene of my brother's suicide alone, without the comfort of my wife and son.

"Do you want to stay a little longer?" he asked finally.

"No," I told him.

I gave Warren a final glance, then followed Peak back down the stairs and out into the yard where we stood together in the misty light that swept out from the school playground. The air was completely still, the scattered leaves lying flat, like dead birds, in the unkempt yard.

Peak looked over toward the playground, and I could see how troubled the sight of it made him, the fear he had that some other little girl was still in peril because whoever had taken Amy Giordano was still out there.

"I read that leads get cold after a couple of weeks," I said.

"Sometimes."

"It's been two weeks."

He nodded. "That's what Vince Giordano keeps telling me."

"He wants his daughter back," I said. "I can understand that."

Peak drew his gaze over to me. "We're testing the cigarettes. It takes a while to get the results."

"And what if they were Keith's?"

"It means he lied," Peak said. "He told Vince Giordano that he never left the house. He said he was inside the whole time."

"And he was," I said, a response that struck me as wholly reflexive.

Peak returned his attention to the deserted playground, held his gaze on the ghostly swings and monkey bars and seesaws. He seemed to see dead children playing there.

"What if your son hurt Amy Giordano?" He looked at me very intently, and I saw that he was asking the deepest imaginable question. "I mean, if you knew he did it, but also knew that he was going to get away with it, and that after that, he was going to do it again, which most of them do, men who kill children. If you knew all that I've just said, Mr. Moore, what would you do then?"

I would kill him. The answer flashed through my mind so suddenly and irrefutably that I recoiled from this raw truth before replying to Peak. "I wouldn't let him get away with it."

Peak seemed to see the stark line that led me to this place, how much had been lost on the way, the shaved-down nature of my circumstances, how little I had left to lose. "I believe you," he said.

———

Meredith was waiting for me when I got home, and the minute I saw her, I recalled the way she'd stood with Rodenberry, and all my earlier feelings rose up, hot and cold, a searing blade of ice.

"He's dead," I told her flatly.

Her hand lifted mutely to her mouth.

"He shot himself in the head."

She stared at me from behind her hand, still silent, although I couldn't tell if it were shock or simply her own dead center that kept her silent.

I sat down in the chair across from her. "What did he say to you?"

She looked at me strangely. "Why are you so angry, Eric?"

I had no way to answer her without revealing the murky water in which my own emotions now washed about. "The cops will want to know."

She bowed her head slightly. "I'm so sorry, Eric," she said quietly. "Warren was so—"

Her feelings for Warren sounded like metal banging steel. "Oh please," I blurted. "You couldn't stand him."

She looked stunned. "Don't say that."

"Why not? It's the truth."

She looked at me as if I were a stranger who'd somehow managed to crawl into the body of her husband. "What's the matter with you?"

"Maybe I'm tired of lies."

"What lies?"

I wanted to confront her, tell her that I'd seen her and Rodenberry in the college parking lot, but some final cowardice, or perhaps it was only fear that if I broached that subject, I would surely lose her, warned me away. "Warren's lies, for one thing. Those pictures the cops found on Keith's computer. They were Warren's."

Her eyes glistened slightly, and I saw how wracked she was, how reduced by our long ordeal, her emotions tingling at the surface.

"Leo told me about it," I went on. "He said Warren had been caught watching kids play at the elementary school. He'd stand at the window of his little 'bachelor lair' and watch them. With binoculars. It was so fucking obvious the school complained about it. The principal went over and told Warren to stop it. So when this thing with Amy Giordano happened, somebody called the police hotline and told them about Warren."

"So that's what it was," Meredith said. She seemed relieved, as if a small dread had been taken from her. She remained silent a moment, gazing at her hands. Then she said, "Warren couldn't have done something like that, Eric. He couldn't have hurt a little girl."

Her certainty surprised me. She had never cared for my brother, never had the slightest respect for him. He was one of life's losers, and Meredith had never had any patience for such people. Warren's drinking and self-pity had only made it worse. But now, out of nowhere, she seemed completely confident that Warren had had nothing to do with Amy Giordano's disappearance.

"How do you know?" I asked.

"I know Warren," she answered.

"Really? How can you be so sure you know him?"

"Aren't you?"

"No."

"He was your brother, Eric. You've known him all your life."

Peak had said the same thing, and now I gave the same reply. "I'm not sure you ever know anyone."

She looked at me, puzzled and alarmed, but also alerted to something hidden. "Warren said you came over to his house. He said you had a quarrel."

"It wasn't exactly a quarrel," I told her.

"That's what he called it," Meredith said. "What was it then?"

"I talked to him about the pictures."

"What did he say?"

"That they weren't really sexual." I shook my head. "He said he just liked looking at the pictures. That the kids were . . . adorable."

"And you didn't believe him?"

"No."

"Why not?"

"Oh come on, Meredith, he fits the profile in every aspect. Especially the low self-esteem part."

"If low self-esteem is a big deal, then you'd better mark Keith for a pedophile, too."

"Don't think that hasn't crossed my mind."

Now amazement gave way to shock. "You think that?"

"Don't you?"

"No, I don't."

"Wait a minute," I yelped. "You're the one who first had doubts about Keith."

"But I never thought it was a sexual thing. That even if he hurt Amy, it wasn't because of sex."

"What then?"

"Anger," Meredith answered. "Or maybe a cry for attention."

A cry for attention.

This sounded like the sort of psychobabble that would come from Stuart Rodenberry, and I bristled at the thought that Meredith was arguing with me through him, using his professional expertise and experience against me.

"Oh, bullshit," I said sharply. "You don't believe a word of that."

"What are you saying, Eric?"

"I'm saying that from the minute Amy disappeared you thought Keith was involved. And I don't for a fucking second believe you thought a 'cry for attention' had anything to do with it." I looked at her hotly. "You thought it was in the family. Something he inherited. Connected to me. To Warren." I laughed brutally. "And you were probably right."

"Right? You mean because you've decided that Warren was a pedophile?" Her gaze was pure challenge. "And what, Eric, makes you so sure of that? A few pictures on his computer? The fact that he liked to watch kids play? Jesus Christ, anybody could—"

"More than that," I interrupted.

"What then?"

I shook my head. "I don't want to go into this anymore, Meredith."

I started to turn away, but she grabbed my arm and jerked me around to face her. "Oh no, you don't. You're not walking away from this. You accuse Keith of being a pedophile, a kidnapper, and God knows what else. You accuse me of suggesting that something awful is in your family. You do all that, and then you think you can just say you're tired and walk away? Oh no, Eric, not this time. You don't walk away from an accusation like that. No, no. You stand right here and you tell me why you're so fucking sure of all this bullshit."

I pulled away, unable to confront what I'd seen in Jenny's room that morning, then conveyed to Warren in a single glance, how, upon that accusation, he must have finally decided that the world was no longer a fit place for him.

But again Meredith grabbed my arm. "Tell me," she demanded. "What did Warren or Keith ever do to—"

"It has nothing to do with Keith."

"So, it's Warren then?"

I gazed at her desolately. "Yes."

She saw the anguish flare in my eyes. "What happened, Eric?"

"I thought I saw something."

"Something . . . in Warren?"

"No. In Jenny."

Meredith peered at me unbelievingly. "Jenny?"

"The day she died I went into her room. She was trying desperately to tell me something. Moving all around. Lips.

Legs. Desperate. I bent down to try to hear what she was saying, but then she stopped dead and pulled away from me and just lay there, looking toward the door." I drew in a troubled breath. "Warren was standing at the door. He'd been with Jenny that night and . . ." I stopped. "And I thought maybe he—"

"Jesus, Eric," Meredith gasped. "You said that to him?"

"No," I answered. "But he saw it."

She stared at me as if I were a strange creature who'd just washed up on the beach beside her, a crawler of black depths. "You had no evidence of that at all, Eric," she said. "No evidence at all that Warren did anything to your sister"—there was a lacerating disappointment in her gaze—"How could you have done that? Said something like that without . . . knowing anything?"

I thought of the way she and Rodenberry had stood together in the parking lot, their bodies so close, the cool air, the night, the rustle of fallen leaves when the wind touched them. "You don't always need evidence," I said coldly. "Sometimes you just know."

She said nothing more, but I felt utterly berated, like a small boy whipped into a corner. To get out of it, I struck back in the only way that seemed open to me.

"I saw you tonight," I told her.

"Saw me?"

"You and Rodenberry."

She seemed hardly able to comprehend what I was saying.

"In the parking lot at the college."

Her lips sealed tightly.

"Talking."

Her eyes became small, reptilian slits. "And?" she snapped. "What are you getting at, Eric?"

"I want to know what's going on," I said haughtily, a man who knew his rights and intended to exercise them.

Fire leaped in her eyes. "Wasn't Warren enough for you, Eric?" she asked. "Isn't one life enough?"

She could not have more deeply wounded me if she'd fired a bullet into my head, but what she said next was said with such utter finality that I knew nothing could return me to the world that had existed before she said it.

"I don't know you anymore," she added. Then she turned and walked up the stairs.

I knew that she meant it, and that she meant it absolutely. Meredith was not a woman to make false gestures, bluff, halt at the precipice, or seek to regain it once she'd gone over. Something had broken, the bridge that connected us, and even at that early moment, when I was still feeling the heat of her eyes like the sting of a slap, I knew that the process of repair would be long, if it could be done at all.

TWENTY-FIVE

Warren was buried on a bright, crisp afternoon. My father had told me flatly that he had no intention of going to the funeral, so it was only the strained and separating members of my second family, along with a few people Warren had gotten to know over the years, regulars at the bars he frequented, who came to say good-bye to him.

Meredith watched stiffly as the coffin was lowered into the ground, Keith at her side, looking even more pale and emaciated than usual. He'd reacted to Warren's death by not reacting to it at all, which was typical of Keith. Standing at the grave, so small a force beside the tidal wave of his mother, he looked incapable of weathering any of life's coming storms. I could not imagine him ever marrying or having children or adequately managing even the least complicated and demanding aspects of life.

When the funeral was over, we walked out of the cemetery together, Meredith's body so rigid, her face so stonily composed, holding down such sulfuric rage, that I thought she might suddenly wheel around and slap me.

But she didn't, and so, as we all passed through the gate of the cemetery, I suppose we looked like a normal family, one whose members shared grief and joy, made the best of whatever life sent our way.

At least that is certainly how we appeared to Vincent Giordano.

He was standing outside his delivery van, its door oddly open, as if in preparation for a quick getaway. His eyes were no longer moist and bloodshot, not at all like the day he'd approached me outside the photo shop. He stood erect, rather than stooped, and there was nothing broken or beggarly in his posture. He pulled away from the van as we approached our car, his body rolling like a great stone toward us.

I looked at Meredith. "Get in the car," I told her, then turned to Keith. "You, too."

By then Vince was closing in.

"Hello, Vince," I said coolly.

Vince stopped and folded his large beefy arms over his chest. "I just came to tell you it won't work."

"I don't know what you mean."

"That brother of yours shooting himself," Vince said. "It's not going to get that son of yours off the hook."

"Vince, we shouldn't be having this conversation."

"You heard what I said."

"It's in the hands of the police, Vince. And that's where it should be."

"You heard what I said," Vince repeated. "That kid of yours is not going to get away with it. You can hire a fancy lawyer, do whatever else you want to, but that kid is not going to get away with it." His eyes flared. "My little girl is dead."

"We don't know that."

"Yes, we do," Vince said. "Two weeks. What else could it be?"

"I don't know," I said.

He looked over my shoulder and I knew he was glaring at Keith.

"They found his cigarettes at Amy's window," Vince said. "Outside her window. He said he didn't leave the house. So, whose cigarettes are they, huh? Tell me that. Why did he lie, tell me that!" His voice rang high and desperate, reaching for heaven. "Tell me that. You or that fancy lawyer you hired to protect his fucking ass!"

"That's enough," I said.

"It's your whole goddamn family that's screwed up," Vince screamed. "A brother watches kids in the playground, looks at dirty pictures of little kids. That's where that son of yours got it from. The family. In their blood." He was seething now. "You should all be wiped out!" he cried. "Every goddamn one of you!"

I felt his hot breath on my face, turned quickly, strode to my car, and got in. For a moment we locked eyes, and I saw how deeply Vince Giordano hated me, hated Keith, hated the neat little family he'd watched come through the cemetery gate, the kind of family he'd once had and which had been taken from him, he felt certain, by my son.

We drove directly home, Meredith trembling all the way, terrified that Vince would follow us there. From time to time, she glanced at the rearview mirror, searching for his green van behind us. I had never seen her so frightened, and I knew that part of her fear was that the husband she'd once trusted had changed irrevocably.

At home, she wanted me to call the police, but I had leaped to so many conclusions of late, that I refused to leap to another one.

"He's just upset," I told her. "He has a right to be."

"But he doesn't have a right to threaten us," Meredith cried.

"He didn't threaten us," I reminded her. "Besides, the police won't do anything. They can't unless he does something first."

She shook her head in exasperation, no doubt convinced that here again I was simply refusing to confront the obvious truth that Vince Giordano was a dangerous man. "All right, fine," she snapped, "but if anything happens, Eric, it's on your head."

With that, she stormed down the corridor to her office and slammed the door.

I built a fire and for a long time sat, staring at the flames. Outside, autumn leaves gathered and blew apart at the will of the wind. The gray air darkened steadily, and night finally fell. Yet Meredith remained in her room, and Keith in his.

It wasn't until early evening that one of them, Keith, finally joined me in the living room.

"So, are we not going to have dinner?" he asked.

I drew my eyes from the fire and faced him. "Nobody feels like cooking, I guess."

"So, what does that mean . . . like . . . we don't eat?"

"No, we'll eat."

"Okay."

"All right," I said. I got to my feet. "Come on, let's go get a pizza."

We walked out of the house and down the brick walkway, past the shadowy limbs of the Japanese maple.

The drive to Nico's took only a few minutes, and on the way, Keith sat on the passenger side, looking less sullen than before, as if he were beginning to emerge from the tiresome irritation of his teenage years. A light played in his eyes, a hint of energy, or perhaps some spark of hope that his life might one day be less plagued with trouble. I recalled a line I'd read somewhere, that we must be able to imagine redemption before we can achieve it.

"I'd ask you how things are," I said. "But you hate that question."

He looked over at me and a faint smile fluttered on his lips. "I was going to ask you that. I mean, Mom's really mad at you, right?"

"Yes, she is."

"What about?"

"She blames me for being too suspicious."

"Of her?"

"Of everything, I guess," I answered. "I have to try harder, Keith. I have to get more evidence before I jump to conclusions."

"What were you suspicious about?"

"Just things."

"So, you won't tell me?"

"It's between your mother and me," I said.

"What if I told you something. A secret."

I felt a chill pass over me.

"Would you tell me then?" Keith asked. "Like, an exchange? You know, father and son?"

I watched him closely for a moment, then decided that where I'd gone wrong with Keith was in failing to recognize that despite his teenage aloofness, the sullen behavior that fixed him in an angry smirk, there was an adult growing inside him, forming within the brittle chrysalis of adolescence, and that this adult had to be recognized and carefully coaxed out, that it was time to confront not Keith's immaturity, but the fact that he was soon to be a man.

"Okay," I told him. "An exchange."

He drew in a long breath, then said, "The money. It wasn't for me. And what I told Mr. Price—about running away—that wasn't true."

"What was the money for?"

"This girl," Keith said. "We're sort of . . . you know. And she has it really bad at home, and I thought, okay, maybe I could get her out of it. Get her away from it."

"Am I allowed to know who this girl is?" I asked.

"Her name is Polly," Keith said shyly. "She lives on the other side of town. Those walks I go on. At night. That's where we meet."

"The other side of town," I repeated. "Near the water tower."

He looked surprised. "Yes."

I smiled. "Okay, I guess it's my turn. This thing with your mother. The things she's so mad about. It's that I accused her of having a lover." I felt a tight ball of pain release its grip on me. "I didn't have any evidence, but I accused her anyway."

He looked at me softly. "You believed I hurt Amy Giordano, too."

I nodded. "Yes, Keith, I did."

"Do you still think that?"

I looked at him again and saw nothing but a shy, tender boy, reserved and oddly solitary, fighting his own inner battles as we all must, coming to terms with his limits, which we all must do, struggling to free himself from the bonds that seem unnatural, find himself within the incomprehensible tangle of hopes and fears that is the roiling substance of every human being. I saw all of that, and in seeing that, saw that my son was not the killer of a child.

"No, I don't, Keith," I said. Then I pulled the car over and drew him into my arms and felt his body grow soft and pliant in my embrace and my body do the same in his, and in that surrender, we both suddenly released the sweetest imaginable tears.

Then we released each other and wiped those same tears away and laughed at the sheer strangeness of the moment.

"Okay, pizza," I said as I started the car again.

Keith smiled. "Pepperoni and onion," he said.

Nico's wasn't crowded that night, and so Keith and I sat alone on a small bench and waited for our order. He took out a handheld video game and played silently, while I perused the local paper. There was a story about Amy Giordano, but it was short and on page four, relating only that police were still in the process of "eliminating suspects."

I showed the last two words to Keith. "That means you," I said. "You're being eliminated as a suspect."

He smiled and nodded, then went back to his game.

I glanced outside, toward the pizza delivery van that rested beside the curb. A deliveryman waited beside the truck. He was tall and very thin, with dark hair and small slightly bulging eyes. He leaned languidly against the front of the truck, smoking casually, and watching cars pull in and out of the parking lot. Then suddenly he straightened, tossed the cigarette on the ground, hustled into his van, and drove away.

"Pepperoni and onion," someone called from behind the counter.

Keith and I stepped up to get it. I paid for the pizza, handed it to Keith, and the two of us headed for the car. On the way, I glanced down to where the deliveryman had tossed his cigarette. There were several butts floating in a pool of oily water. All of them were Marlboros.

———

I kept that fact to myself until we reached the exit of the parking lot. Then I stopped the car and looked at Keith. "The night you ordered pizza for you and Amy, did you order it from Nico's?"

Keith nodded. "Where else?"

"What did the guy who delivered it look like?"

"Tall," Keith said. "Skinny."

"Did you happen to see the guy who was standing outside the delivery van a few minutes ago?"

"No."

"He was tall and skinny," I said. "Smoked one cigarette after another."

"So?"

"He smokes Marlboros."

Keith's face seemed to age before my eyes, grow dark and knowing, as if the full weight of life, the web of accident and circumstance in which we all are ensnared, had suddenly appeared to him.

"We should call the cops." he said.

I shook my head. "They've probably already checked him out. Besides, we don't even know if it's the same guy who came to Amy's house that night."

"But if it is," Keith said. "He might still have her."

"No," I said. "If he took her, she's long dead by now."

Keith was not convinced. "But what if she's not. Shouldn't we at least try?"

"We have nothing to go on," I told him. "Just that a guy who delivers pizzas from Nico's also happens to smoke the kind of cigarette you smoke, along with millions of other people. Besides, like I said before, the police have already questioned him, I'm sure."

I couldn't be certain that Keith accepted my argument, but he said nothing more, and we went the rest of the way home in silence.

Meredith was in the kitchen when we arrived. We set the table together, then sat talking quietly, and during those few minutes I came to believe that for all the terrible disruptions our family had suffered during the past two weeks, we might yet reclaim the normal balance we had once possessed. I wanted to believe that Meredith's anger toward me might dissipate as Keith's resentment had seemed to dissipate, that we might regain our common footing as a family, if for no other reason than that we were all simply too exhausted by events to hold each other at knifepoint any longer. Anger takes energy, I told myself, and unless its devouring fire is steadily and continually stoked, it will cool to embers soon enough. It was for that reason perhaps more than any other that I decided simply to let things go, to say nothing more about Amy Giordano or Warren or Rodenberry, to hold back and wait and hope that after Amy Giordano had finally been found and the shock of Warren's death and the accusing finger I'd so recklessly pointed at Meredith had grown less painful, we might come together again as a family.

After dinner, Keith went to his room. From below, I could hear him pacing about, as if worrying a point, trying to come to a conclusion. Meredith heard him, too, but said nothing about it, and so the source of Keith's anxiety never came up that evening.

We went to bed at just before ten, Meredith's back to me like a fortress.

"I love you, Meredith," I told her.

She didn't answer or turn toward me, but I hoped that in the end she would—that in the end we would survive.

She went to sleep a few minutes later, but I remained awake for a long time before finally drifting off.

By morning, Meredith seemed slightly less brittle, which gave me yet more hope. Still, I didn't press the issue, but instead remained quiet and kept my distance.

Keith left for school at his usual time, and a few minutes later I went to work. The day passed like most days, and I reveled in the simple uneventfulness of it. Keith got home at just after four and found a message on the phone, telling him that I'd decided it was time for him to start making deliveries again. He got on his bike, peddled to the shop, and gathered up the deliveries for that afternoon. There were a lot of them, but I had no doubt that he'd still be able to get them done and get back to the shop before I closed for the day.

It was nearly six when I finally closed the shop and headed for my car; at almost that very same moment, Vincent Giordano had locked the front door of his produce market, then picked up his cell phone and called his wife, telling her not to worry—he'd be home before the news.

Y̲ou see it suddenly, the face. It swims toward you out of the crowd, so utterly clear and distinct and achingly recognizable that it blurs all other faces. It drifts toward you with wide, searching eyes and streaming hair, like a head carried in a crystal stream. She lifts her hand in greeting when she sees you seated in your booth beside the window. Then she moves down the aisle toward you, a face you have not seen in years and remember most from the flyer you taped on the window of your shop, a face that seemed to hang from a jagged fence of big black letters—MISSING.

"Thank you for doing this, Mr. Moore," she says.

"I would do anything for you, Amy."

She is twenty-three, her face a little fuller than before, but with the same flawless skin. You see that she is adorable, your mind returning, after so many years, to the word Warren used, and from which you judged him suspect in crimes both near and distant.

"I'm not sure what I'm looking for," she says.

She draws a dark blue scarf from her head and lets her hair fall free. It is shorter than it was then, with no hint of wave, and you recall how it fell well below her shoulders the last time she was in your shop. You remember the penetration with which she peered at the cameras on display, as if touching the knobs and dials with her inquiring mind.

"I'm getting married, I suppose that's part of it," she says. "I just want to . . . settle everything before I start a family of my own."

She waits for a response, but you only watch her silently.

"Does that sound crazy?" she asks. "My wanting to talk to you?"

"No."

She peels off her raincoat, folds it neatly, and places it on the seat beside her. You wonder if she's going to pull out a notebook, begin to take notes. You're relieved when she doesn't.

"I've told Stephen everything," she says. "Stephen's my fiancé. Anyway, I told him everything about what happened. At least, everything I remember." She sits back slightly, as if you are giving off waves of heat. "Maybe I just wanted to say thank you."

"For what?"

"For noticing things," she says. "And for doing something about it."

I recall the sound of Keith's footsteps in his upstairs room, his soft tread across the carpet, back and forth, back and forth, how, during those lonely minutes, he must have been trying to decide what he should do, weighing what I'd earlier told him, weighing it all the next day before finally dismissing it, and in that fateful dismissal, becoming for all time a man.

"I didn't do anything about it," I tell her.

"Yes," she says. "That was Keith."

"Only Keith."

I see what I could not have seen at the time. I see my son at school, see him glance at the pay phone in the lunchroom, stop, think it through again, then dial the number he'd seen posted on flyers in the school lobby and on shop windows throughout the town, a number used for rumors, wild notions, false sightings, vicious gossip, unfounded suspicions, and occasionally, very occasionally, the shattering possibility of salvation. I hear the voice, which I had always judged weak and irresolute, but which now sounds powerful in my mind, forceful, confident, determined.

"I just wish it had all happened before"—her eyes hold the immemorial regret of our kind, the iron door that closes with each movement of the second hand—"I want to tell you how sorry I am."

Her father's words echo in my mind—*I'll be home before the news.*

What had he meant by home? I wonder suddenly. Had he meant the house he'd shared with his wife and daughter? Or had it been some other home he expected to reach, the place where he hoped to find peace, or at least forgetfulness?

"It was all so terrible," she says. "So unfair. Especially since Keith had already called the police."

You hear your son's voice, hear it as clearly as when Peak played it for you three days later.

"This is Keith. Keith Moore, and last night my dad and I went for pizza at Nico's and we saw a man who might have delivered pizza to Amy Giordano's house that night, and he smokes Marlboro cigarettes, and I just think you should at least go talk to him because, you know, well, maybe it's not too late . . . for Amy."

Now images rise from the gray depths. You see the man taken into custody, a little girl carried up basement stairs and out to a waiting ambulance, her long dark hair tangled and matted with filth, one eye swollen shut, her lips parched and cracked. You hold this image in your mind as you stare at the face that faces yours, healed by time, the lips moist, hair immaculately clean and neatly combed.

"He would have killed me really soon," she tells you. "He'd already dug the grave."

You have no doubt that this is true, that had your brave and noble son not made his lonely, lonely choice, Amy Giordano would be dead.

"I only wish I could have thanked Keith."

Now the final hours of your family life pass before you in a series of photographs that were never taken, but which you have carried all these years in the grim portfolio of your mind. You see Keith on his bicycle, pedaling back from his deliveries. You see him turn into the parking lot, holding one leg out as he always did, the photo shop in the background. You see him coast down the hill toward the shop, a green van now entering the frame. You see the slender barrel inch from the van's open window, a hunting rifle, complete with scope. You see your son in the crosshairs, his arm lifted, waving to you as he hurtles toward the shop, where you stand, staring helplessly, until the awful sound reverberates, and your son rises from the seat of his bike, rises as if rudely jerked from it by an invisible hand and hurled backward onto the dark pavement where he lies writhing as you run toward him.

"I don't know why he did it," she says. "My dad."

You see yourself in pictures now. You see yourself collapse beside your strangely still son, gather his lifeless body into your arms, then shudder as another shot rips the otherwise ghostly silent air, and your eyes dart toward the sound, and you see a second body, slumped over the wheel of Vincent Giordano's green van.

"He did it," you say, "because he loved you."

Her eyes glisten, and for a moment the two of you flow one into the other and become a single, irremediable ache.

"I'm sorry, too," you tell her.

And it's true, you are sorry for Amy, and for Karen who never married again, and for Meredith who could not hold on to anything after Keith's death, could not live with you or even in the town where you'd made a family and briefly a good life, and so she had drifted first to Boston and then to California and then to some third place from which she has sent no word.

"Well," Amy says, "I just felt that I wanted to see you and tell you how sorry I am for everything that happened." She shakes her head. "There was just so much . . . misunderstanding." She starts to get up.

"No, wait," you tell her.

She eases back into the seat and peers at you quizzically.

"I want to talk to you," you tell her. "You're getting married, about to have a family of your own. There are things, Amy, you need to know."

She nods. "I know there are," she says.

"I'd like to help," you tell her. "Give you the benefit of what I've learned."

"Okay," she says, then waits, ready to receive whatever gifts you have.

You think of Warren, Meredith, Keith, the family you briefly held, then doubted, and finally lost. You recall your final glimpse of your house, the winding walkway that led from the driveway to the front door, the sturdy grill, the Japanese maple you'd lovingly planted so many years before, how on that final day you'd glanced at the ground beneath it, so baffled now, so tormented by doubts and suspicions that you could no longer tell whether you saw a pool of blood beneath its naked limbs or just a scattering of red leaves.

You close your eyes, then open them, and all of that is gone, and you see only Amy.

"I'll start at the end," you tell her. "The day I left my house."

And then, as in a family photograph, you smile.